St. Elizabet

Dealing with sick kids can be heartbreaking,
funny and uplifting, often all at once!

This series takes a look at a hospital set up
especially to deal with such children,
peeping behind the scenes into almost all the
departments and clinics, exploring the problems,
treatments and cures of various diseases,
while watching the staff fall helplessly in love—
with the kids and with each other.

Enjoy!

As a person who lists her hobbies as reading, reading and reading, it is hardly surprising that **Meredith Webber** fell into writing when she needed a job that she could do at home. Not that anyone in the family considers it a "real job"! She is fortunate to live on the Gold Coast in Queensland, Australia, as this gives her the opportunity to catch up with many other people with the same "unreal" job when they visit the popular tourist area.

A WINTER BRIDE
Meredith Webber

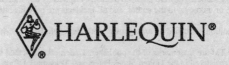

HARLEQUIN®

TORONTO • NEW YORK • LONDON
AMSTERDAM • PARIS • SYDNEY • HAMBURG
STOCKHOLM • ATHENS • TOKYO • MILAN • MADRID
PRAGUE • WARSAW • BUDAPEST • AUCKLAND

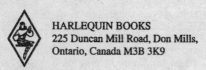

HARLEQUIN BOOKS
225 Duncan Mill Road, Don Mills,
Ontario, Canada M3B 3K9

ISBN 0-373-63159-6

A WINTER BRIDE

First North American Publication 2001

Copyright © 2000 by Meredith Webber

This edition published by arrangement with Harlequin Books S.A.

® and TM are trademarks of the publisher. Trademarks indicated with
® are registered in the United States Patent and Trademark Office, the
Canadian Trade Marks Office and in other countries.

Visit us at www.eHarlequin.com

Printed in U.S.A.

CHAPTER ONE

FLAPPING her arms to the chorus of farewell, and with more awkwardness than grace, Nicole hopped backwards out of the door of the small meeting room where the pre-schoolers' clinic had been held, slap-bang into a bulky body. As her oversize shoes threatened to catapult her to the floor, firm hands gripped her waist and held her upright, while a deep voice, more than faintly reminiscent of dark chocolate, muttered, 'What the hell?' in the vicinity of her ear.

She regained her balance and turned to see Mark Gregory grinning at her from the other side of the corridor and a tall stranger struggling to remove his feet from under the elongated toes of her clown shoes.

'Nicole Barclay, David Campbell. David, meet Nicole. Last therapy session she was a fairy. Can your mind make the stretch to a strapping wench of five-ten or so in tinsel and spangled wings? No? Well, don't bother. It was a particularly gruesome sight. Come on in and meet some normal members of the team.'

Mark performed this most perfunctory of introductions, added his little joke then ushered the newcomer through the door, leaving Nikki gaping after them.

After him.

Not Mark, but the newcomer.

David Campbell.

The name was already etched on her heart, as the image of the tallest, most gorgeous-looking man she'd met in years was imprinted on her mind.

He's probably married, she told herself as she shuffled

towards the washrooms to change back into regular working clothes. And even if he isn't, he must be attached. Men with hair the colour of a raven's wing, eyes as blue as Mediterranean skies, and bones a sculptor would die to make immortal weren't left on the shelf. Men like that had women queuing up to take their turn; flocks of women panting after them; hordes of women—mostly short.

'It's utterly unfair,' she said, addressing Crystal, the occupational therapist on their team, who was renewing her make-up in front of the washroom mirror. 'Short women have so many men to choose from they should leave the tall ones for those of us who aren't vertically challenged.'

'You're prejudiced,' Crystal retorted. 'And you should be ashamed of yourself. You're always going on about that "woman can do anything" credo. These days women are dating younger men, older women marrying their toy boys, so what's wrong with a tall woman and a shorter man?'

'There's nothing wrong with it. I go out with shorter men all the time, but it would be nice to feel protected now and again, to have a chap hold an umbrella over me instead of me over him.'

Crystal chuckled.

'Trouble with Alan?'

Nikki sighed.

'No, not really. In fact, that's the problem. I guess if I cared enough to have trouble with him, if we argued, or fought, or even disagreed occasionally, it might prove there's some spark there. He's just so *nice!*' She emphasised the adjective but knew it still hadn't conveyed quite what was lacking in their relationship. 'I told him I didn't think there was any point in our pursuing it. So I'm back on the shelf—again.'

'I don't know what you're looking for in a man,' Crystal complained. 'If they argue with you they're opinionated, and if they don't argue, they're too nice! Perhaps the right one hasn't happened along just yet.'

'Perhaps!' Nikki echoed, while a startlingly clear picture of blue eyes and raven-dark hair flicked onto a screen in her head.

She pulled off her red nose, peeled back the wig with its attached clown's hat and threw the lot into an old cricket bag of her brother's, then stripped off the shoes, trousers and floppy shirt and faced herself in the mirror. She was perfectly proportioned with broad shoulders, a good bust, neat waist flaring out to curving hips, and long, strong legs to carry her effortlessly through the day, but size ten she wasn't.

Cute she wasn't.

Petite wasn't even a dream.

'Mark just introduced me as a strapping wench,' she said gloomily. 'Can't really blame him, can I?'

'Junoesque might be a kinder description,' Crystal offered.

'Kinder than what? Elephantine?' Nikki snorted as she pulled on her jeans. 'And even though he is my brother and no earthly good to me as a marriage partner, you still had no right to take Peter out of circulation instead of leaving him for someone who needed his superior height.'

'So he could hold an umbrella over her head? Forget it! Wear a raincoat!'

Crystal, apparently satisfied with her make-up repairs, darted out of the room before Nikki could throw the hairbrush she'd picked up.

Returning the hairbrush to the bag, she buttoned the bright smock she wore over her jeans, and slathered cold cream on her face, watching as the coloured clown face dissolved into a mess of black, red and white smears.

'Laugh, clown, laugh!' she muttered to herself, mopping

at the mess with tissues. 'Or at least put this bout of self-indulgent moodiness down to PMT.'

She washed her face with soap and water to remove what was left of the make-up, then dried it, plastered moisturiser on and grimaced at her reflection. Her shoulder-length ash-blonde hair, thanks to its recent confinement under the wig, hung limply around her face, her grey-green eyes were rimmed with red from the make-up and cream, and her clear pale skin was shiny with moisturiser. She'd certainly have been more noticeable to David Campbell in the clown's suit than in real life.

Though she doubted she'd see him again. Their team was complete, no new staff on the horizon, so he must be a visiting dignitary of some kind, taking a guided tour of the paediatric rheumatology unit, an adjunct to the outpatients department at Lizzie's. Or he might be doing the full St Elizabeth's Children's Hospital tour—with Mark deputed to showing him Outpatients and the arthritis unit.

Perhaps he was an old friend of Mark's. Someone from his student days, passing through London, looking him up.

Not staying even if he was available.

'Cripes, Nicole, get your act into gear here!' She struck herself lightly on the side of her head with the flat of her hand, hoping to jolt her mind off the man she'd met so fleetingly. Perhaps jar the image of smouldering blue eyes and midnight-dark hair from her head. And had his eyes actually smouldered?

She doubted it. She must have made that part up.

With a sigh that echoed futilely around the room, she shouldered the big bag and made her way back along the corridor to Outpatients, where she dumped it under the desk in the office she shared with Crystal and Pat Knowles, a paediatric nurse seconded to the unit.

Paperwork awaited her, reports on the children she'd seen that morning to be typed up, then she had to review all their exercise programmes and probably revise half of them. Some children improved faster than she expected, some progressed more slowly. Her aim was to structure each individual programme to challenge the particular child, without stretching his or her capabilities too far. There was a delicate balance between the achievable and the impossible, and psychological factors to consider as well. Achieving goals brought pleasure and pride while striving for the impossible decreased self-worth.

She was working on Jamie Blythe's programme when a voice interrupted her thoughts.

'You're wanted up on the orthopaedic ward.' Claire Oates, who was Mark's secretary but stood in as message-taker for all those in the unit, put her head around the door. 'Something about that boy who had his knuckle joints replaced.'

'That "boy" is a teenager of sixteen with systemic JRA, who once dreamt of playing cricket for England.'

'Systemic as in all over?' Claire asked. 'I thought juvenile rheumatoid arthritis was usually just that, juvenile, and most kids grew out of it.'

'*Most* kids do,' Nikki told her. 'But for some, especially those with the systemic version, the disease has caused so much damage to the joints they'll never recover from the crippling effects of it, or be free of pain in the damaged joints. Tom Crowley, the lad in question, is one of those.'

'So, he'll never play for England.'

Claire sounded so upset, Nikki walked to the door and patted her on the shoulder.

'No, but I'm steering his mind more towards being a commentator, and he quite likes that idea.'

'But how many people get jobs like that?' Claire demanded. 'Aren't you putting false hopes into his head? Setting him up for more disappointment?'

'No, I'm not,' Nikki said fiercely. 'Everyone needs a

dream to reach for, something to strive towards. It's not
having a dream, a goal, that leads to depression and a sense
of worthlessness. Even if he doesn't make it, he'll at least
have the satisfaction of knowing he tried.'

She walked along the corridor towards the lifts, then
turned back to Claire.

'But he won't fail!' she added. 'Not Tom.'

As she entered the lift and nodded to fellow staff, she
repeated the words in her head. She might have sounded
confident about Tom's chances of success when she spoke
to Claire, but knew there were no certainties in life.

Was she wrong to feed him dreams?

The lift disgorged her at the orthopaedic floor and, still
thinking about her patient, she headed towards his bed at
the far end of the ward. Technically he could have been
treated as an adult and in an adult facility but he'd been
coming to Lizzie's since he was diagnosed with JRA at
three, and a more regular visitor since his joint mobility
began decreasing when he was nine.

Lizzie's was a second home to him, and it would have
been hard to send him somewhere else for this latest op.

'Well, hi there, Tommo. You got problems, man?'

She pushed open the curtains as she spoke, thinking he'd
drawn them, as he sometimes did, to retreat from the
younger patients who regarded him as their guru.

And walked slap-bang into a bulky body.

Again.

Worse still, it was the same bulky body—the man who,
no doubt, now mentally labelled her not only 'the strapping
wench' but 'clumsy dolt' as well.

'Er, sorry. I thought Tom would be on his own in here.
It's late for ward rounds. Are you okay?'

She manoeuvred around the stranger and addressed the
last question to Tom, who was sitting up in bed scowling
at Mark.

Tom gestured towards the specialist who was standing on the opposite side of the bed.

'He *says* the operation was successful, but look.' The teenager raised his hand to show raw scars and swollen fingers—crooked swollen fingers.

Nikki looked, and with a sick sinking in her heart realised what he meant. For some reason, he'd imagined the joint replacement would make his fingers straight again—make him 'normal'.

'Tom, you had the joints replaced to stop the pain. You knew that was why you were having the operation.'

He turned his scowl on her.

'I'd rather have the pain and straight fingers. If they can replace knuckles why can't they do that?'

'Maybe, one day, they will be able to do it,' she said, deciding brisk was best in this situation. 'But in the meantime, you can sit there and brood over life's unfairness, and feel thoroughly sorry for yourself, or you can decide to work with what you've got and start exercises to extend your range of motion with those fingers. You've got three weeks before the Lord's Test, and if you want to sit in the broadcasting box you've got to be useful, which means keeping a computerised score. Means using those fingers, Tom.'

'The Lord's Test? Broadcasting box. This is cricket you're talking about?'

The dark chocolate voice slicked over her skin on its way to insinuate itself into her ears.

'What else?' Tom said, all but dismissing the man's questions as he challenged Nikki. 'You've arranged it? I can go?'

'If you can type again by then,' she warned him. 'But don't push yourself too hard until your wounds heal. Just gentle range-of-motion exercises, a few minutes at a time.'

'He's going to sit in the broadcasting box at the Test?'

The stunned disbelief in the lovely voice snagged Nikki's attention, and she swung to face the visitor—to look into the deep-ocean blue of his eyes.

'Are you a fan?' she asked, surprised to find her mouth was working when everything else in her body had stopped dead: heart, lungs, stomach, all gripped by a strange sensation—as if she'd stepped off the end of the world.

'Fan? You could say that. I planned this trip to coincide with the test series and I'm hoping to get along to Lord's, but to get into the broadcast box, mate...'

His attention swung back to Tom.

'If I was given an opportunity like that, I'd forget I had crooked fingers and get cracking on my exercises.'

The word 'mate' was a clue, and now she listened she could hear the faint echo of an Australian accent in the melodious voice.

'Okay for those who haven't got crooked fingers to say forget them,' Tom muttered at him, but as Nikki watched the teenager moved his hands, gingerly stretching his fingers as far as the stitches and swelling would allow.

She wondered what to do next, her body so aware of David Campbell, her mind busy coping with the messages bombarding it, she couldn't think straight.

Work—she'd concentrate on that.

'You wanted to see me, Tom?'

'No!' He snapped the word at her, so unlike his usual cheery self she realised how deeply upset he must be. 'It was him had you paged.'

He jerked his head towards Mark.

'Suits me,' Nikki said easily. 'Don't push those fingers while they're still swollen. I'll be up at the usual time in the morning.'

She dodged around the body causing her so much internal strife and through the curtains, but escape wasn't going to be that easy. The body caught up as she left the ward, his hand landing squarely on her shoulder, not only halting her progress, but spinning her around.

'That kid's upset. According to Mark, you handle him better than anyone. That's why he called you up. Aren't you going to do something?'

Maybe his voice wasn't so much like dark chocolate as she'd at first thought—unless you counted chocolate with razor-blades embedded in it.

She squared up to him and met those eyes—hard sapphires, not soft skies.

'Like what? Cry over his twisted fingers? Tell him fairy tales he won't believe anyway? Carry on about all the people worse off than he is? It would be an insult to his intelligence—which is formidable—to go on with such meaningless blah. In fact, he'd think less of me if I did and I've worked damned hard to win Tom's respect.'

'But he's shocked. Surely it's someone he does respect who could help him over this new disappointment.'

Was he right?

She considered what she knew of Tom's personality, and shook her head.

'No. Now he's blown off a bit of steam, he'll work through it on his own. Mark was right, you know. Tom knew exactly what the operation was for—the straight fingers must have been a bit of wishful thinking that sneaked in under his defences. Or perhaps it's the aftermath of the anaesthetic—a kind of gloomy hangover. He's usually far more practical about his prognosis.'

The look she got was cool and disbelieving, but as Mark arrived at that moment she couldn't challenge this uppity antipodean to prove her wrong about a patient she'd known for years, and whom he'd only just met.

'Ah, sorry about that, David,' Mark said. 'Usually our patients are quite happy with their repair jobs—anything to be free from pain. Did you talk to Nikki about her dropping you home?'

'I can take a taxi.'

'Me dropping him home?'

They spoke together, but, even so, Nikki heard enough of the intonation in David's voice to know she wasn't his first choice of chauffeur.

'Nonsense.' Mark was having none of it. 'She lives about a half a mile further on and has to drive right past the square. She'll be happy to oblige.'

I will?

She nodded in response to Mark's assurances but refused to show a 'happy' face.

'I've some programmes to finish before I leave. Half an hour suit you?'

The other victim of Mark's organisational skill looked anything but 'suited' by the arrangement, but before he could protest again Mark had taken him by the arm and was bustling him away to his office for a 'quick drink before you go'.

'I'll send him down to your cubby-hole in half an hour,' Mark added over his shoulder, and Nikki was left watching the two retreating backs, one slim and slight, the other tall and broad, more like a rugby forward than a cricket enthusiast.

'Neanderthal!' she muttered to herself, repeating her eldest brother's scornful description of front-row forwards.

But visualising him as a caveman failed to dampen her interest in him as a man—in fact, there was something quite exciting about a caveman with compelling blue eyes and stunning good looks.

She contemplated hitting herself on the head again, and decided she'd look foolish, so meekly made her way back down to Outpatients where she shut herself in the office and completed the exercise programmes, printed them out, and put them into envelopes ready to drop into the postbox as she left the department. The families would have them by the following morning.

David Campbell was standing outside her door when she walked out of the office, and it was only sheer luck that she hadn't swung the cricket bag into him, colliding for the third time in their short acquaintance.

He lifted it from her grasp, swinging it easily onto his shoulder before she could utter a protest.

'Which way?' he asked.

Which way what? she thought blankly as she gazed into the mesmeric eyes.

'To your car,' he added helpfully, the chocolate voice no longer meltingly smooth—more crackly, cold. Refrigerated chocolate?

'It's in the basement—down in the lift—over here.'

She stuttered out the words then led the way, wondering why the man was throwing her off balance—mentally as well as physically. Actually, she could understand the physically—he was gorgeous and it was purely hormonal—but surely her physical and mental selves had worked individually in the past, her mind unaffected by cavorting hormones?

The lift doors slid open and she stepped out into the gloom of the underground car park.

'This way.'

She walked off without waiting to see if he was following, still working on regaining her mental balance. Not that she had a hope of losing him. His strides carried him effortlessly along beside her, and when she used the remote to unlock her car door he stepped ahead to open and hold the driver's side door for her.

'You want your handbag in the back seat or the boot?'

'Huh?'

'Your handbag? In the back seat or will you pop the boot lock and I'll tuck it in there?'

He dangled the cricket bag from his fingers as he repeated the question, and all she could think was how strong those long, lean fingers must be to hold the weight of it so easily.

'Back seat!' She managed to sound almost normal as she answered, then even better when she remembered her manners and added, 'Thank you.'

He shut her door, opened the back and slung the bag on the seat, then walked around the car and climbed in beside her, immediately reducing the interior space to sardine-tin proportions.

'Hmm, more leg room than I expected. I drive a Land Rover Discovery these days—find I'm comfortable in it without getting the feeling that I'm driving a tank.'

What was she supposed to say? That's nice?

She decided his comment didn't need a reply and backed carefully out of the space. After bumping into him twice, she didn't want to compound his impression of her clumsiness with a dented bumper bar.

She made it safely through the boom gates and out on to the main road, edging into the traffic streaming homewards.

'So, where do you live, exactly?' she asked.

He recited off his address like a child who'd been made to memorise what to say by over-anxious parents.

Nikki whistled softly.

'Posh, eh?'

'It's an exchange arrangement,' her passenger said stiffly. 'The owners are staying in my sister's home in Sydney.'

'And where's your sister?'

He turned to look at her, as if startled by her question.

'She's here with me.'

Nikki drove on, wondering why a man his age was travelling with his sister, wanting to ask but not wanting to seem pushy.

He let the silence lie between them for a few minutes, then turned towards her.

'From the way Mark spoke, you make a habit of dressing up for therapy sessions. Do you get better results that way than you would spending the available time on regular therapy? Actually treating the children rather than playing with them?'

The questions were not only unexpected, but asked in a tone that said he didn't need an answer—he'd already made up his mind her 'play' was ineffective.

Nikki ignored them, and her defensive flutter of indignation, easing the car across two lanes of traffic so she'd be in position to turn when she came to the short street leading into the square where he was staying. Once safely into the left lane, she glanced towards him and found him watching her as a scientist might watch a programmed animal.

Waiting for an answer?

'Who exactly are you?' she asked, wondering how her body could possibly be attracted to such an irritating man. 'And how much do you know about paediatric rheumatology?'

'I'm a paediatric specialist and lecturer in rheumatology at the University of New South Wales. I was co-author with Mark—'

'The series of articles in the *British Medical Journal*!'

If he hadn't been sitting right there beside her, she'd definitely have slapped her head again. Why hadn't his name rung a bell?

Because her response to him had been physical rather than cerebral!

Oh, dear!

The silent wail failed to help, but thankfully the turn was just up ahead. She could drop him off and probably never see him again. She knew his and Mark's collaboration had been carried on by e-mail. The man was over here to watch some cricket and had just popped in to meet Mark in person and see the hospital and the unit. That way he could probably write the cost of the trip off his tax.

'You haven't answered my questions about your therapy sessions,' he reminded her.

'I thought you were just making conversation,' she said, remembering the flicker of indignation his questions had raised.

'I rarely bother making conversation. I was asking because I'll be doing Mark's job for the next month or so and understand his position includes responsibility for all the treatment in the unit.'

'Mark's job? Responsibility?' The words fluttered from her lips, made breathless by the squeezing of her lungs and sudden pounding of her heart. 'Where's Mark going? Why hasn't he said anything?'

She found enough composure to make the left-hand turn, then another to the right which took her into the square with its fenced garden in the middle and tall white houses guarding the perimeter.

'Does he usually share his personal arrangements with all the staff?'

'This isn't personal, it's work!' Nikki pointed out, slowing as she tried to find a house number—and rein in her temper. 'And we're not employed under a feudal hierarchy at Lizzie's, Dr Campbell, we work together as a team. Has the concept of teamwork reached Australia yet?'

'It's the next one,' he said, ignoring her tirade and pointing towards a newly painted building, its classy black door gleaming in the light thrown by an old brass coach lamp.

She stopped the car in front of the steps leading up to

the stylish entrance, her mind racing as she tried to make sense of this astonishing news.

He opened the car door, but hesitated before alighting.

'Thanks for the lift. I'll see you tomorrow. I gather you have a regular unit meeting on Thursday mornings. I assume Mark will introduce me to all the staff then. But in the meantime you can take it that I'm right, and if you prefer not to answer now I'll wait until I'm officially your boss.' The blue eyes seared into her. 'Tomorrow.'

'But Mark can't just leave like that!' The protest burst from her lips as anxiety over what had prompted the sudden decision melded with apprehension about working with this man—sinfully appealing though he was.

'He has to ask your permission?'

The dry question skated along her nerves, alerting some inner intuitiveness to suggest something badly wrong.

'The tests! Mark's been having a series of blood tests.' She stared at the stranger's face, fear chilling any licentious thoughts she might have had earlier. 'Cancer?'

David Campbell's face revealed nothing.

'Mark will explain tomorrow.'

Nikki reacted without thought, gripping the infuriating man's shoulder and making a futile attempt to shake him.

'I don't want to know tomorrow. I want to know now, damn you. What's wrong with Mark? Is it bad or curable? You can't say that much then walk away, leaving me prey to the worst nightmares my brain can conjure up. Besides, if he tells us tomorrow in the meeting and it's really bad, I'll cry, I know I will, and women my size look stupid crying.'

For a moment she thought he was going to ignore her pleas, but she held her tongue while his eyes scanned her face as if trying to read her mind—perhaps gauge how she'd react if he refused to say more.

'It's not cancer,' he said bluntly. 'Why on earth would

you leap to that conclusion and get all hysterical about it? Whatever happened to British reserve? Stiff upper lip?'

Relief for Mark made her smile although his little daggerish insults had pierced her skin.

'I didn't get it,' she explained glibly. 'The reserve and reticence. I guess it came from growing up with three brothers then realising being a girl put restrictions on me. I hated it, always demanded to know why.'

'And argued, kicked and screamed even when the reason was quite logical.'

She stopped smiling. He was guessing, she knew, but that didn't stop him being right. Not that she was going to admit it. He was too full of his own importance already.

'So where's he going? Mark, I mean.'

For a moment she thought he wasn't going to tell her, shifting in the seat as if discussing someone else's business made him physically uncomfortable.

'How well do you know him? Know the family?'

The family! Light dawned and she felt a smile of pure delight spread across her face.

'Anna's got the job! The part in the film. And she's panicking about going off to the fleshpots of Hollywood on her own and he's going with her. Oh, David, that's so wonderful. I'm so glad for her and for Mark, who's always encouraged her with her acting, so this is his reward as well. If I wasn't sitting down I'd dance a jig, I'm so excited.'

'I did detect a modicum of excitement,' David said dryly, detaching her hand which had gripped his suit coat and been shaking it as she spoke. 'Can you dance a jig?'

She clutched the steering wheel to stop her hands wandering again and answered automatically, wondering at the same time why he hadn't got out and walked into his house.

'Of course I can,' she said. 'Dancing lessons were part of my mother's campaign to convince me I was going to grow up female instead of male. She had some idea that dancing at Covent Garden might become an alternative goal in my life. Mind you, she never aspired to the Royal Ballet for me, but thought maybe a smaller company…'

'And what was your goal? What had you set your sights on?'

He sounded more puzzled than interested, Nikki decided, while she wondered if she'd answer him. Part of her wanted to keep him in the car because she was fascinated by him, attracted to him, wanted to learn all she could about him.

The other part reminded her of all the reasons the attraction was illogical and warned her to steer clear of him and his physically disturbing body.

Perhaps if he thought she was a complete idiot, he'd steer clear of her—save her the bother.

'It was the same as Tom's. To play cricket for England.'

He didn't look aghast at the suggestion, merely more puzzled.

'Weren't you good enough? I understand there are women's test teams. Didn't you make the grade?'

Remembered frustration boiled through her blood again, and she was sure the scorn she felt was reflected in her eyes.

'I didn't want to play women's cricket,' she said heatedly. 'I wanted to play in the real team, with my brothers.'

His lips twitched as if he was trying not to smile—which was fortunate for him as she didn't consider it a laughing matter. Then they steadied and he said, in his detached way, as if her answer really held no interest for him, 'And did they play for England? Your brothers?'

'One did,' she admitted gruffly. 'But only for one season because in the end he decided cricket was something he could do for a few years, whereas medicine was something he could do for ever. With the professional approach these days, it's hard to do both. My younger brother, Gerald, could make it, could be a top cricketer. He's only seventeen so he has to finish school then decide if he wants to make a career of it. If anything, he's better— I'm rattling on, aren't I? It's the lack of reticence again. I'll let you go. It was very kind of you to step into the breach when Mark wanted to go away.'

There, she could be polite when she made the effort.

'To put off a couple of days at the cricket for a colleague who needed a break? Yeah, that was a real big deal.' He drawled out the words, exaggerating his Australian accent. 'But don't count on the kindness shining through in the work environment. Thanks for the lift, Miss Barclay.'

He pushed the door open and climbed out, shutting it gently but firmly behind him and striding up the steps to his shiny front door without a backward glance.

CHAPTER TWO

DRIVING to work was usually a pleasurable activity, as Nicole left her home in leafy Hampstead early to avoid the worst of the traffic, and could spend the time thinking about the day ahead of her, planning something special for the children she saw regularly, working out ways to make their boring, repetitive exercises more fun.

But today, the closer she got to the hospital, the less pleasant it became, although she told herself things wouldn't change just because Mark was away for a few weeks. He would want the team to carry on as usual. In fact, they could have run the unit without him for such a short time.

Perhaps she'd tell him that, explain that his friend really wanted to watch cricket and relax, not work in a strange place with people he didn't know. Yes! Mark was usually as early as she was—she'd talk to him before anyone else arrived.

The thought buoyed her enough to drive in through the boom gate instead of using her mobile to call in sick.

'Good morning, Miss Barclay.'

Her car door swung open and the words sounded like a death knell in her ears. So much for catching Mark on his own!

Well, perhaps it was time to fall back on the old English reserve—time she learned it anyway. Just be cool and calm at all times in the man's presence.

'Good morning, Dr Campbell,' she said politely as she clambered out in the restricted space between vehicles. She

found she was speaking to his back as he had opened the
rear door as well and was peering into the back seat.

'No props today?' he asked as he straightened up and
looked down into her face.

Reticence, she reminded herself. Don't bite.

'No pre-schoolers,' she said, shrugging one shoulder to
show him his slighting remark hadn't affected her.

Although his body had. The strange energy it radiated
was enveloping her, and, while her feet might not be dancing a jig, her intestines certainly were. Yes, definitely time
she learned to hide her emotions.

'You've got a car today?'

It was an inane remark when he'd obviously just got out
of the gleaming black Range Rover parked beside her car.

'My sister hired it yesterday. Not that she intends driving, she informed me, but so I can drive her places at week-
ends.' He hesitated, and Nikki thought she caught a gleam
of humour in his eyes, although in the dimly lit car park it
was hard to tell. 'She's about as delighted over my taking
Mark's place for a few weeks as you are, Miss Barclay. I
think she thought I'd be happy to act as chauffeur for the
entire time we're in London. Driving her back and forth to
Harrods, I assume.'

Nikki was so puzzled by the role of his sister in his life
she ignored the jibe about her not wanting him working on
the team.

'And your wife? Does she drive?'

The twinkle, if ever it had existed, disappeared, and his
eyes darkened as if a shadow had fallen across them.

'I don't have a wife.'

He turned and strode towards the lifts, leaving Nikki to
haul her briefcase out of the car, lock it, then follow, trailing after him like an abandoned puppy.

At least he held the lift for her, although travelling with
him in the metal cubicle was nearly as bad as having him

sitting in her car, as far as proximity to his body was concerned.

He stood back so she could exit first, then walked behind her towards the offices. Her door was the closest and she stepped inside, shut it behind her and slumped against it, dropping her briefcase to the floor and holding one hand to her chest in the hope that external pressure might calm her erratic heartbeats.

'Is the big bad wolf chasing you?'

Crystal's voice levitated her a foot into the air.

'What on earth are you doing here at this hour of the morning?' Nikki demanded. 'You nearly gave me a heart attack, speaking to me like that.'

'I thought you were already having a heart attack,' her sister-in-law said. 'The way you were standing there, barricading the door and shaking at the same time. My car's in for a service so I came in with Peter. What's your excuse?'

Nikki frowned at her. Her heart had settled but breathing was still difficult, and understanding conversations obviously beyond her.

'My excuse for what?'

Crystal shook her head.

'You've got it bad, kid,' she said in a sympathetic voice. 'Whoever's rattling your hormones at the moment must be really special. I haven't seen you this shaken since Bono from U2 signed your bra.'

A brisk knock at the door prevented Nikki from voicing a vehement denial. In fact, the interruption had come just in time to save her from some outright lies, and she stepped forward so she could open it.

David Campbell filled the frame and she didn't need to hear Crystal's barely breathed, 'So that's it,' to know what she was thinking.

'Do you want something?' she demanded of David, then

wished she'd tried for a more gracious tone, although she was reasonably sure the gracious gene was closely associated with those of reserve and reticence, and hadn't come to her. 'I'm not officially at work, but if you've got a problem…'

There, that was better, though not much if Crystal's snort was anything to go by. Which reminded her of manners. She did have those—they were learned, not inherited.

'This is Crystal Barclay, our occupational therapist.'

She stepped aside to perform the introductions, muttered his name for Crystal to hear, then watched his double take as he assimilated diminutive Crystal's beauty, and linked their surnames.

'You're sisters?'

'In-law,' Crystal said, standing up behind her desk and offering him her hand and a dazzling smile. 'How do you do? My husband, Peter, was telling me you'd agreed to take Mark's place while he's away. I do hope you enjoy your time at Lizzie's. We're a friendly lot. Peter's on the surgical staff here, so you'll meet up with him eventually.'

That's why she's in early, Nikki decided bitterly. She knew he was coming and wanted to impress him.

Daggers of jealousy she'd never felt towards Crystal, not even when she'd married her favourite brother, struck deep into Nikki's intestines.

Not that Crystal needed to try to impress men. All she had to do was lift her melting brown eyes in their direction and toss her glossy brown hair, and they fell in line to worship at her feet.

'I'm going up to the ward to see Tom, then check on who needs adjustments to their programmes,' Nikki announced, breaking into a conversation that sounded like an open house invitation from Crystal to this man she'd only just met. What had happened to *her* reserve and reticence?

'Good, I'll come with you,' David said, cutting off that

line of escape. 'I came to ask you if you were seeing Tom this morning. Actually, there's something I'd like to talk to him about, but Mark said to discuss it with you first. He seems to feel you know the lad better than anyone.'

'Then stay here and talk,' Crystal suggested. 'I put the urn on when I arrived so the water's hot if you want tea or coffee. I have to see the technicians about a new plastic for splints so you'll have the office to yourselves until Pat arrives.'

Feelings of jealousy gave way to a sense of betrayal. What was Crystal doing, leaving her alone with the man?

Nikki picked up her briefcase, crossed the room to her desk, scuttled behind it as if it might provide some protective barrier against his seductive influence, and finally faced him. He pulled the chair from in front of Crystal's desk and set it across from her, then said, 'Coffee or tea?' as if he were the host and she the guest.

She stumbled to her feet, all but knocking over her own chair in the process. Seeing her clumsiness, he'd never believe the dancing lessons!

'I'll get it. Which would you prefer? And we've biscuits.' She pulled open the door of the small cupboard that was their pantry and grabbed the biscuit tin. 'Oatmeal or oatmeal, by the look of things.'

'Coffee, black, no sugar, and no biscuit, thank you.'

He was doing 'reserved' much better than she was.

She made his coffee and decided she'd forgo the pleasure as she was likely to slop it everywhere if she did have a cup. She set his on the desk in front of him, then settled back into her chair.

Control, that was what was needed here. And a little professionalism.

'You wanted to talk to me about Tom?'

She breathed deeply when those blue eyes met hers. Control was easier when she wasn't looking at him—when he wasn't looking at her.

'I wanted to talk to you about my talking to Tom,' he corrected. 'Did you read any of the articles Mark and I collaborated on—apart from the authors' names?'

She didn't flinch. That would be to acknowledge he'd scored another hit with his glib tongue.

'You debated the use of corticosteroids, more aggressive drug therapy, earlier on in the treatment of paediatric arthritis. I know Mark still favours traditional methods of NSAIDs, the non-steroidal anti-inflammatory drugs, and aspirin for the reduction of swelling during flares.'

'And you? How do you feel? You see the crippling effects of joint deterioration, the long-term effect of it not only on the joints but on the person's life in general. Would you prevent that if you could?'

She could hear his commitment in his voice and feel an added excitement, as if he radiated the strength of his convictions, but she couldn't agree for the sake of agreeing.

'Not all children suffer crippling effects. What is it these days? About eighty per cent of JRA sufferers go on into adulthood with no permanent damage. You can't treat all children aggressively and take the risk that corticosteroids may affect their general long-term health in other ways, when eighty per cent of them recover anyway,'

'So you'd let the twenty per cent suffer—become crippled like Tom—without even offering them an alternative?'

Nikki frowned at him. How could she possibly be attracted to a man who needled her at every opportunity?

'You came in here to talk about Tom, and all you've done is hammer me with questions. Obviously, we need more research so we can work out which kids are likely to be in the twenty per cent who won't recover fully.'

'Or give them a choice?'

He stood up as he spoke and began to pace back and forth across the limited space.

'That's what I'd like to discuss with Tom. You said he's highly intelligent. Is he willing to talk about the disease? About the effect it's had on his own life?'

'He's willing to talk about it, but how can he know what choice he'd have made? It's hypothetical now—too late for him. And with his joints already affected, isn't he likely to say he'd have gone for early aggressive treatment?'

'Not if he's capable of understanding the long-term effects of corticosteroids. Prednisone can affect the eyes, causing cataracts or even glaucoma. It leads to weight gain, elevated blood pressure and high cholesterol which are all danger signals for heart disease.'

'So you'd be offering a life that might be outwardly normal but limited in length because of the unseen damage treatment could cause? Quality or quantity—make a choice!'

The idea didn't sit well, although she'd ached for children who had been crippled by the disease, felt the pain of crippled teenagers who so hated to look different from their peers.

'It isn't a matter of asking him what he might or might not have chosen, but of debating it with him. Trying to see it from a sufferer's point of view. I've spoken to adults who have been left affected, some badly affected, but they'd all come to terms with the results of the disease so thought differently. From what I saw of Tom, he's still working through it.'

'Debating it with him would be okay, I guess.' Nikki agreed reluctantly because she knew who'd be acting intermediary in these 'debates'. Not Mark, who'd be in Hollywood, probably lunching with George Clooney! 'Do you want me to talk to Tom first or will you put it to him?'

David studied her for a moment before replying.

'I think I should speak to him directly, but perhaps with you there so he doesn't feel threatened. If he agrees I'll arrange a time to talk. I guess it's up to you, and him, whether you sit in or not.'

He didn't actually *say* he didn't think she'd learn much from the exercise, but he definitely gave that impression. So much so she forgot her annoyance with Mark for landing her in this situation and heard herself telling Dr Campbell that she'd certainly be interested in being present.

'Tom knows my hands-on schedule, so he can arrange times around that,' she added, then realised she'd doomed herself to more time in David Campbell's unsettling presence when she should have been trying for less.

If only he weren't quite so good-looking. If his eyes weren't quite so blue—

'Shall we go?'

His question jerked her back to the present and she looked up from a lopsided sun she was doodling on her desk blotter and met the same interrogation in his blue eyes.

It took an effort to bite back the 'go where?' that hovered on her tongue and she stood up again and walked towards the door, hoping her brain would click into gear before he realised she'd lost the plot.

Tom! That was it. They were going up to see Tom.

Another lift ride—more proximity. Perhaps being with him would dull the effect of the bombarding rays he emitted, at least cushion her reaction to each glance from those lethally beautiful eyes.

They were alone in the lift this time too—an unusual occurrence in the hospital at any time. She sneaked a look at him, standing tall and straight, eyes focussed on the doors—as reserved and reticent as she should be, their roles reversed.

No, she could do it. Act as cool as he did, pretend her

body wasn't thrown into complete chaos by his, resist bumping against him when the lift jolted to a stop—

Bumped hard against him as it jolted so suddenly she had to grab at his arm for support.

'Rough ride,' she muttered, stepping quickly away, wondering why the doors hadn't opened. Then the lights went out.

'Does this happen often?'

His voice—amused or just bored?—wrapped around her.

'It's never happened to me before. Not ever. It can't happen. This is a hospital. There are generators for reserve power, they cut in automatically, take over as the power goes off. You can't have power going off in operating theatres, or ICUs, anywhere in a hospital—'

She jumped as something brushed her arm—something that turned into a warm, firm hand, gripping her forearm now, steadying her.

'I do understand about generators and the need for continuous power in hospitals,' he said, definitely amused now. 'I'd say it's a malfunction in the lift rather than a power cut, and I've pressed the emergency button. Is it the dark that's bothering you or being stuck in a small enclosed space?'

She sensed him moving closer but resisted the urge to fling herself at him, seeking security, or at least temporary oblivion, in his arms.

'If it *was* small enclosed spaces, your pointing out that's where we are would be a big help!' she said, hoping he'd recognise scathing tones when he heard them. 'And dark has never been a fear for me.'

So far so good. Very calm—very stiff upper lip.

Then she heard a craven voice so soft she barely recognised it as her own.

'I'm not so keen on plummeting to the bottom of a lift well, though. Not good on heights, tall buildings, planes, that kind of thing. I'd rather lifts didn't malfunction while I was in them, because the plummeting downwards always seems more likely when they're not working.'

She heard him chuckle and felt his hand move up her arm and slide around her shoulder until he could draw her close against his body, providing warmth, if not oblivion, and a million other tiny messages he was unaware of sending.

'It's spiders with me. I know I'm bigger than them and can squash them with the slightest pressure of my shoe, but the thought of coming on one unawares is enough to make my blood curdle.'

'You don't have to offer up a weakness to make me feel better,' Nikki told him, certain the reserved man who needled her was easier to resist than a nice version. And while she was on the subject of resistance—

She pushed away from him, finding the rail that ran along the sides of the lift and grasping it to steady herself in the mind-distorting blackness.

'You'd rather we argued while we waited to be rescued? Well, that's okay with me. Perhaps we could go back to my question yesterday about your antics in the therapy sessions. That's almost sure to lead to an argument unless you have unlimited time and money to spend on therapy services over here.'

To think she'd wished for needling!

'My antics, as you call them, work. I've two years of figures to prove it, if you want to see them. We're talking infants and toddlers here, little ones who are too young for formal programmes. What they need is general activity, to be encouraged to run and jump and play, using their muscles naturally.'

'And being dressed as a clown achieves this?'

The disbelief in his deep voice scorched across her skin and, if she'd been able to see his face, she might have wanted to slap it. Although there was probably a hospital rule about physiotherapists slapping the face of visiting specialists...

'Most people know how limited a pre-schooler's attention span is. I can stand in front of these kids and ask them to raise and lower their arms, run and walk and hop, push and pull things across the floor, all that stuff, but it's boring after about twenty seconds because it's what they do at home, every day, over and over again. It's much harder for parents to keep coming up with new ideas.'

'Isn't giving them new ideas your job?'

Nikki was sorry the darkness meant he couldn't see the glare she gave him.

'Of course it is. But how many new ideas are there? At least by having fun sessions at the hospital the parents have something to use as a reward for diligent exercising. Even two-year-olds try harder if they think they might be the one chosen to go first behind the clown, or fairy, or whatever I happen to be.'

'First behind the clown?'

Was he interested or simply testing her, wanting her to prove she did something worthwhile at these sessions?

'Like "follow the leader",' she explained. 'Or whatever other game we play. It's joining in that makes it fun for the kids and they do their exercises without realising what's going on.'

She should explain that she also saw each child individually during the time between joint sessions but he'd been so quick to judge her she didn't bother. He could find that out for himself.

'And older children, what games do you play with them?'

'Do you really care?' she asked. 'Or, knowing I missed out on reserve and reticence, are you quizzing me to keep me from possible hysteria if I brood too much over what might happen in this lift?'

'I'd really like to know,' he said, and she sensed he would, although she also thought she heard a smile in his voice.

Not that you could hear smiles. Except perhaps in total darkness.

'I try to challenge them. The lower school ages are fairly easy. Most of them can be persuaded to keep their joints mobile and their muscles strong, or to work to regain motion and strength in a joint. You've got bribery—pizzas or McDonald's if they've done well all week. Financial and physical rewards—you can't ride a new bike if your knee's not working. As long as they understand that the exercises aren't optional. That they're like teeth-cleaning, something that has to be done every day. Then you reward results.'

'And for older children, teenagers?'

'Ah, they're difficult—mainly because they don't want to be different. So you have to work out a whole new strategy for each individual, and be prepared to alter it every time there's a setback—like Tom's reaction to his joint replacements.'

'You treat every teenager differently?'

She could sense a change in his tone, not disbelief this time, but not avid interest either.

'I treat every child differently as far as their individual programme is concerned. Not all need knee exercises! But adolescence brings so many other problems, coping with stiffness or, worse, deformity, can be totally overwhelming—more than they can handle on top of everything else. And they're too old, know too much, to accept platitudes. Or most of them are.'

'Like "God only gives us the burdens we can carry"? That kind of thing?'

'Exactly,' Nikki said, warming to the man again, mentally warming now. Her body was still battling the invasive heat his presence generated. 'It's a truism, like thinking of those worse off than you are, and, although this kind of mental support works for a lot of people a lot of the time, it doesn't make their stiffness go away, or the deformity of crippled joints any less visible to others. Adolescent self-esteem is tied so inextricably to how others view them—particularly their peers—the outward signs of arthritis are soul-destroying.'

'You said it!'

His agreement was as hearty as it was unexpected, but before she could question the statement the lights came on, the lift jolted, then began to rise again towards the orthopaedic floor.

He was looking at her, his eyes, soft like the sky again, scanning her face, drawing her into them until she felt she were drowning in the blueness.

'Are you okay?' he asked, the question so unexpected she straightened up and gave him her best haughty look—one she usually reserved for pushy people on the tube.

'Of course.'

The doors opened and she stepped away from the supporting rail, then felt her knees buckle as reaction set in. A firm hand gripped her elbow, steadying her for a moment, then easing her forward, out of the lift, and through the small cluster of worried-looking people who all began to babble at once.

'No, we've got no idea what happened,' she heard David say, and she slipped out of his grasp but did turn and smile at him, thankful he was there to stop her pitching headlong into the crowd, pleased he was able to answer questions as she seemed incapable of speech.

'It's shock,' she heard him murmur to her alone. 'Aftermath of a bad experience. Is there somewhere you can sit down? Get a hot drink?'

'No, I'm okay,' she managed to say. 'I'm not shocked. Quite okay.'

But she wasn't. And it wasn't shock. She knew that much.

And she knew what it was, too, this sick-in-the-stomach feeling that seemed to invade her entire being. Knew the symptoms from the first time it had happened. She'd been sixteen and Peter had brought a friend home from Oxford. A friend who'd had a smile like sunshine, and had made Nikki wish she were beautiful.

She'd felt all weak and fluttery back then. Hot and cold at the same time. Happy and sad, confused and impatient, breathless and unsettled. She'd hung on his every word, followed him around like a spare shadow, and generally made a nuisance of herself until he'd told her, very gently, that she was a little young for him.

His gentleness hadn't helped the pain, nor had it plastered up the cracks in her heart, which had taken so long to heal she still felt faint flutters when she saw him at family celebrations.

Then, of course, there'd been Jack, who'd had exactly the same effect on her, only then she'd been older and imagined this was IT. True love. Her knight in shining armour. She'd plunged recklessly into his arms, then into his bed, then plummeted out of the dream four months later when his wife had returned from a photographic safari she'd been on, and reclaimed her husband.

Shame that she could, inadvertently, have caused another woman harm had added to Nikki's devastation and loss. It had also made her determined not to be swayed by her hormones—not ever again. She'd stuck with dating pleasant men who didn't send her body into hot and cold confusion, didn't make her skin tingle or her heart leap or her breathing go haywire. She'd decided friendship was a better basis for a relationship and hoped eventually to find a friend who'd prove a compatible lover as well.

It seemed to have worked quite well, and, although the friend who'd turn into a lover hadn't yet materialised in her life, she was content with the way things were going.

Until now.

When she'd got it again.

Not measles, or mumps or something that would run its course.

But love, which would stay around like an ache in her heart for so long she'd begin to wonder if it would ever go away.

'Bother!' she muttered.

'I beg your pardon?' David Campbell said.

Nikki scowled at him.

'I said bother!' she repeated. 'And if I wasn't so well brought up I'd add a couple of other words.'

She spun away from his startled gaze, and strode back towards the lifts. There were washrooms just beyond them. She'd splash her face with water, perhaps put her head under the tap. Do something to bring her senses back under control before she had to sit with the cause of all her problems and try to behave like a rational human being.

CHAPTER THREE

IT COULDN'T be, Nikki told her damp reflection. She looked pale so perhaps it was the flu. Or bubonic plague. That would be good—she'd be duty-bound to go home right now so she didn't infect anyone else during the incubation period, and stay home at least a month.

Or however long Mark intended being absent from his post.

And she'd have something to say to him, too. Supporting his wife was one thing, but throwing this man into their team was too much.

She blotted the excess moisture off her face with a paper towel, noticed with despair that the paleness had gone, leaving an unmistakable glow of health in its place, and plodded gloomily out of the washroom and back to the ward.

Where she found Tom positively radiant with goodwill.

'Dr Campbell wants me to sit on a panel as a representative for juvenile arthritis sufferers,' he reported excitedly. 'He's studying the effects of different drugs and wants some input from me.'

By the sound of his delight, it beat sitting in the broadcasting box at Lord's any day.

'That's nice,' Nikki managed, keeping her attention fixed on Tom so she could avoid looking at David Campbell. 'And when does all this panel business begin?'

'Oh, as soon as he works out a programme with you,' Tom informed her. 'I told him you're the best of the therapists and other ancillary staff because you see past the disease to the person.'

'Ancillary staff?' Nikki repeated. 'Have you been eating dictionaries for breakfast?'

It was better to make jokes with Tom than consider her inclusion on this 'panel', which would be headed by the wonder doctor himself.

'As I've only a limited time here, I'd like to get on with it,' the wonder doctor said. 'Have you time today for a preliminary discussion of who else we might include? You'd have more idea which parents and teachers would be appropriate to approach.'

Nikki knew she had to face him, had to put aside her irrational reaction to the man, and that included linking chocolate syrup to his voice every time he used it. At this rate, she'd put on weight just being in the same room.

'She has individual appointments up to lunch-time, then a therapy class three-thirty to four-thirty that usually doesn't finish until after five because the parents all ask questions afterwards,' Tom answered for her. 'You could buy her lunch. The canteen's not bad or there's a little coffee shop near the news-stand, if you want more privacy.'

At least turning to berate Tom gave her an excuse to look away from David.

'Are you arranging all my life, or just the Lizzie's section of it?' she demanded, just as David said,

'Lunch sounds good to me. One o'clock? In the coffee shop?'

'I suppose so.' Totally flustered now, she gave in because she was reasonably certain, if bubonic plague wasn't an option, that she wouldn't be able to think of an acceptable excuse.

'See you there, then,' he said, and walked away.

She watched him go, saw him glance at his wrist, then turn back to catch her watching him.

'Did Mark say something about a unit meeting at nine?

Seems we're already late. I'll hold the lift, if you're prepared to risk it again.'

Bloody hell, the unit meeting! Punctuality was one quality she did have. Usually.

'I'm never late,' she told him crossly. 'It's your fault.'

He bowed slightly, as if he took her words as a compliment, then said, 'We could blame the lift malfunction.'

She seized on the excuse.

'So we could,' she said happily, as the same conveyance
took them swiftly to the ground floor. 'What a good idea.'

She was still smiling with relief when they walked into
the therapy room where the weekly meetings were held.
Ten heads turned in her direction, took in her stupid grin,
and the tall, handsome man behind her, then ten expressions
changed from polite interest to knowing smirks.

Crystal's smirk more knowing and more noticeable than
the rest.

Nikki squeezed in beside her, threw her a poisonous
look, then focussed her attention on Mark.

Not a good idea. He was waving David Campbell towards him with an imperious hand, indicating David should
take the vacant seat beside him at the front of the room.

Mark's introduction listed an impressive array of quali-
fications. Perhaps higher degrees were easier to get in
Australia, Nikki thought, then wondered when she'd become so mean-spirited.

And shouldn't she be lapping up this evidence of her
love-interest's brilliance?

No, not when the love-interest was totally unwanted, and
certainly not reciprocal.

'Bono didn't sign my bra, he signed my T-shirt,' she
hissed at Crystal.

'You want to share that thought, Nikki?' Mark asked,
and she felt heat suffuse her cheeks with tell-tale colour.

'The lift broke down,' she mumbled weakly. 'That's why I was late.'

'Yes, David has already told us,' Mark said kindly, then, thankfully, moved on to business, introducing the general hospital staff like the dietitian, psychologist and social worker, who could be called in by the unit staff, the technical staff who made to measure special aids or equipment, the orthopaedic specialist who attended their meetings when he could, and the secretarial staff.

He went on to explain his need to take leave, and assure the team they'd be in good hands with David as their temporary boss.

The analogy made Nikki shiver.

'I think I'm getting the flu,' she whispered to Crystal, deciding it was more believable than bubonic plague, if not as long-lasting.

'You're never sick,' Crystal reminded her, under cover of a question directed to David Campbell. Intent on avoiding looking at him, Nikki also missed the content of the query, catching up when her own name snagged her attention.

'Miss Barclay is already organising a panel of arthritis patients, parents, and possibly staff, to debate the advantages and disadvantages of the use of more aggressive therapy in the initial stages of the disease.'

He bestowed a falsely complicit smile on Nikki then continued to explain his aims and field questions on his opinions of the contentious issue.

Mark then ran through some programme changes, asked for discussion on various patients, explained that David would be sitting in a lot of sessions over the next few working days to get a feel for the place, then dismissed them, departing himself to a chorus of 'good luck's.

'If you need to break a leg for luck in the acting profession, make sure it's yours, not Anna's,' Nikki said to him when she met him outside the room. She kissed him on the cheek in the kind of casual farewell she'd been giving him since he and Peter began their medical training together, then hurried across to her office. She had a new patient due in any minute, and wanted to read through the file once again.

Maggie Thomas, diagnosed with scleroderma—a name that meant, literally, hard skin. In Maggie's case it was localised, and linear—the lesions occurring in lines rather than patches.

She scanned through the files, then headed for the treatment room where Pat was already talking to the little girl and her anxious parents.

'Do you normally give physio to patients with localised scleroderma?'

David Campbell's voice brought her to a sudden halt in the doorway so this time it was he who crashed into her. The effect was the same: strong, firm hands gripping her waist to steady her, starting flutters of butterflies in her stomach.

She managed to step clear of him, and turned so she could answer him without the visitors hearing the conversation.

'If the skin becomes stuck to underlying connective tissue, particularly over a joint, then, yes, I do. This is a new patient, and I haven't examined her, but when Mark suggests someone will benefit from physio he's usually right.'

She turned back and smiled at the people gathered in the room, then, as David showed no signs of departing, she introduced him.

'He's learning how we do things over here,' she added, the nasty jab prompted by her body's reaction to the man.

She then put him firmly from her mind and concentrated on the child, introducing herself, asking questions about school and friends and favourite toys, offering answers herself when the child's shyness reduced her replies to head-shakes and nods. As she talked, she used her hands to tell her what was happening beneath the whitish patches of thickened and swollen skin.

'Does this hurt?' she asked, and saw Maggie's shiny black curls riot about her head as she vigorously shook a 'no'.

'This?'

Another no.

'What happens sometimes,' she said, speaking directly to the child, 'is that the swollen skin catches hold of the bits of tissue underneath it and stops those bits from growing.'

She pressed her fingers into the left knee and felt the constriction of the underlying connective tissue.

'Because of that, Maggie, you're going to have to do a lot of stretching exercises so your knee can keep working properly. And down here, where your muscle is—' she cupped her hand around the small calf muscle '—you have to work even harder so this muscle grows back as big as the one on your good leg. It's not easy, but when you grow up and are twelve or so, and want to wear pretty stockings, you want both your legs to look the same, don't you?'

Maggie nodded enthusiastically enough for Nikki to ignore the snort of derision she imagined she heard behind her. David Campbell was only here for a month; she had to work with this child for the next year at least.

'Now, I've got this cute little tape measure, and I'm going to measure your muscles and your leg today, then measure them again every time you visit me, so we can see just how well you're doing with your exercises. Do you want to hold one end for me?'

Maggie sat up, then chortled with delight when Nikki handed her a beautiful tape she'd fashioned from lace and ribbon. She had one printed with cars and earth-moving equipment for the boys, who always knew exactly which piece of machinery was marking their current progress.

Pat jotted down the measurements as Nikki read them out.

'There,' Nikki told her. 'Now I'll show you a few exercises to help that leg, but the very best thing you can do is walk a lot—up and down steps is especially good. Do you have a bike?'

'It's pink,' Maggie told her, growing bold enough to speak instead of nodding.

'Do you know,' Nikki told her, 'it's a funny thing, but I've found pink bikes are the very best for exercise. You ride that pink bike as much as you can, and when you're in the bath, or in bed at night before you go to sleep, you stretch out your bad leg as far as you can, think about it growing longer and longer like Pinocchio's nose when he told the lies.'

She demonstrated the specific exercises she wanted Maggie to do each day, explaining how they would help improve the child's mobility. Pat, who'd ducked out after the measuring, returned with an individualised folder which she gave to Nikki to check before passing on to the parents.

'My direct number and my home number are on the front page,' Nikki explained. 'If you have any problems, phone me. I'd be only too happy to help.'

'Do you give your home number to all patients?' David asked as the Thomas family departed.

'Of course,' Nikki told him. 'I've done it for years now, and no one's ever abused it. The way I see it, there's no point in having an expert involved in your child's treatment if you can't contact him or her in a crisis. Kids are so vulnerable,' she added, looking into his eyes to make sure he got the point. 'Sometimes a delay of twenty-four hours is about twenty hours too late.'

Twenty hours too late—it was about that for her right

now, she realised as the eyes did her in. If she'd been away yesterday, whatever the configuration of the stars, planets and malevolent fates, which had thrown her into this state, might have changed by today and she could have met this man as a colleague, nothing more. Avoided the onslaught-of-love business altogether.

Although, considering the underlying aggravation he seemed to feel towards her—the prickliness that came through in all his conversations with her—he would be doing some avoiding of his own, which should help.

'Hmm.'

He turned and walked away, leaving her to make whatever she could of the noise. Perhaps more assessing than aggravated?

She headed for her office, then remembered she had another patient due, and after that a child to see up on the ward, a four-year-old in for some physical rehabilitation after a severe and painful flare of JRA.

She was in the heated pool with the hospitalised patient, Sarah Jacobs, splashing and playing after the session finished, when she realised she was supposed to be at lunch with the new boss.

Well, at least he couldn't possibly get the idea she was trying to impress him, she told herself as she dragged a comb through her wet hair and felt the ends dampen the collar of her smock, so it lost its shape and sat askew around her neck.

He was seated at a table towards the back of the coffee shop, and as Nikki wove through the chattering crowd on her way to join him she couldn't fail to notice the covert inspection he was undergoing from every female in the café. And that included two women in their seventies who were part of the volunteer programme of play grannies.

'I'm sorry I've kept you waiting,' she said, slipping into the chair opposite him and telling herself that the way his dark hair made his skin look paler was none of her business.

'Bad hair day?' he asked with mocking sympathy. 'It's an excuse my sister uses all the time.'

'Actually, I've been doing a therapy session in the pool,' Nikki told him, hoping he'd recognise an icy put-down when he heard one. 'Have you ordered?'

He looked startled for a moment, then the blue eyes positively gleamed into hers.

'In Australia, it's polite to wait until the guest arrives before ordering, particularly if the guest—'

'Is having a bad hair day?' Nikki cut in before he could add some fulsome but false compliment. 'I thought this was a business lunch. You wanted to talk about your panel, so talk.'

He seemed disconcerted, which was good because disconcerted was a pale shadow of what she was feeling.

'I'm currently collating all the information I can find on early treatment with corticosteroids versus traditional methods including gold. I've a table showing the early results of the admittedly limited testing undertaken so far. Would that be a good starting point for discussion?'

She was so startled to find him asking her opinion she couldn't reply, but was saved from further embarrassment by the arrival of the waitress.

'I'll have the vegetable lasagne stack and salad and a mineral water,' she said. 'And a pot of English Breakfast tea and scone to follow.'

David seemed surprised by her decisiveness. He ordered toasted sandwiches for himself, then waited until the woman departed before bringing Nikki back to the subject with a slight arching of his beautifully arched eyebrows.

'I think it would be a great starting arch—I mean point,' she said, realising the man must think she was crazy as well as unco-ordinated and unattractive.

Would he have mentioned her hair if he hadn't noticed it?

He nodded, then produced a manilla folder from somewhere out of Nikki's sight—presumably a briefcase on the floor beside his chair.

'These are the figures I have so far, and there's some general background information on the study. I realise it's an imposition for you—' a charming smile accompanied this assertion; one that had probably worked wonders on other women in his past '—but if you could find time to read through it, then consider who, aside from Tom, might be interested in participating.'

Nikki took the folder and set it carefully on the table beside her bread and butter plate, deciding not to look at it until later, in case she dropped the pages into her lunch, or spilled tea over them.

She glanced up and saw him watching her, a slight smile on his lips, almost as if he'd read her thoughts and was agreeing with them. The smile, for whatever reason it had appeared, seemed to lighten the dark handsomeness of his face, making him seem less Hollywood-handsome—more human and approachable.

Except he should have an 'approach me only if you dare' sign around his neck so susceptible females could keep well away.

'Why are you so keen to approve the early use of steroids?' she asked him, using work to oust a few of her more fanciful notions.

'I think it's sad that a disease which so often goes into permanent remission should still have dire long-term consequences for its victims. I'm not talking about patients with the associated diseases like lupus, but the children with the various forms of juvenile rheumatoid arthritis in particular. Those with the most severe forms, like systemic

JRA, can suffer arthritis long after the disease has left their body. For ever, in fact.'

'But—' Nikki began, and he held up his hand. The same hand that had held her arm when she'd begun to worry in the lift.

'I know the buts,' he said. 'The side effects of all the more aggressive drugs, particularly the corticosteroids, are well documented. But because of possible side effects, we haven't used them enough to know if short-term treatment early on can provide a quick cure without the side effects.'

This twist on conventional thinking was new to Nikki, piercing the other distractions in her mind like a ray of light.

'It would be wonderful if something could be proved,' she said tentatively.

'Exactly,' David agreed, and this time his smile spread right across his lips, and sparkled in his eyes, so the fluttering in her heart became acute and the butterflies in her intestines rose in clouds and threatened to choke her. Fortunately lunch arrived at that very moment, and she was able to turn her attention to the meal and hope her foolish, answering grin hadn't been a dead give-away.

'Well, I must say it's refreshing to see a woman enjoy her food.'

His comment, as she was thanking the waitress for removing her empty plate and setting the scone in front of her, made her look up—to see another smile.

'I suppose your sister is one of those reed-thin women who consider a lettuce leaf and a slice of tomato sufficient for lunch.'

The smile widened. Apparently he hadn't heard the tartness in her voice.

'I think she adds an occasional olive,' he said. 'Shall I pour your tea?'

Now don't start being nice to me, Nikki wanted to say.

I'm having enough trouble staying sane when you're needling and provoking me.

But manners won out. And curiosity.

'Thank you,' she said. 'And your olive-eating sister? Does she work?'

'She lives on a generous divorce settlement.'

The statement, so flatly delivered, startled Nikki and she glanced up from spreading a thick layer of jam on her scone and saw that his face had become closed and dark again—the smile no longer lurking in his eyes. Had he been through a similar experience? Was that why he had no wife?

'You don't approve?'

The question popped out before she could vet it, and, once out, hovered in the air between them as David Campbell rearranged the cutlery on the table as if, perhaps, he hadn't heard it.

'No, I don't,' he said at last. 'Her ex-husband worked darned hard to make the money she enjoyed spending, and it irks me he should have had to sell up most of his property to provide for her in such style.' He shrugged. 'But then, it appears he did it willingly. Perhaps he was more anxious to get rid of her than I thought.'

There was sadness in his voice, and it touched Nikki, although she'd been determined not to keep reacting to him.

'You liked him?' she asked, and saw the smile hesitate at the corners of his wide, beautifully moulded mouth.

'Still do—he's far from dead. He was a friend of mine before he married Meg, so I guess I feel partly responsible for the whole mess.'

'Were there children?'

It seemed a natural question to ask, so she didn't expect to see those lips tighten once again, or the man glower across the table at her.

'One daughter,' he said coolly, then he picked up the

folded bill from the centre of the table, added, 'I'm sorry to abandon you like this but I have an appointment with Mark. He leaves tomorrow. Get back to me whenever you can about the panel.'

And with that he departed, leaving Nikki staring after him, wondering why a question about his niece should so upset him.

Given his rapid departure, she didn't expect to see him again that day, but, as if he knew his presence rattled her, he arrived in the big room where she held group therapy sessions just as she was examining the children's reward posters which they kept at home to show how diligently they'd exercised.

'See, Nikki, I got smiling faces every week this month— no sad faces.'

Susan Templeton had been, when Nikki had first met her, the most manipulative child she'd until then encountered, contriving not only to get out of exercises, but to have her parents carry her whenever possible. Now, two years later, she was a delight, working hard at keeping her joints mobile and her muscles strong, and even providing a lot of encouragement for other children in the group.

'It means I get to braid your hair,' Susan added, and Nikki didn't need to see David's eyebrows rise to know how he'd take that remark.

'I can help,' Emma Ricco added. 'I've got smiling faces too.'

'How on earth did I let myself in for this?' Nikki asked Emma's mother, who was laughing at the therapist's dismay. 'You haven't had all smiling faces for two months, Emma.'

'It was the promise we could play with your hair,' Susan told her. 'Emma loves playing with hair. She's going to be a hairdresser when she grows up, aren't you, Emma?'

Nikki thought of the polyarticular JRA already affecting

so many of Emma's joints, the disease five times more prevalent in girls than boys, and wondered if perhaps Emma might have been one child who would have benefited from David's idea of early, more aggressive therapy.

Could still benefit?

She glanced up and found him watching her and wondered again if her thoughts were readable. This time she'd have liked him to know what she was thinking, perhaps tell her if it was too late to consider corticosteroids in Emma's case.

She could ask him later.

'Now, all in position for some general range-of-motion exercises, starting with necks.'

The children slipped into position, some more easily than others, pairing off and facing each other, hands resting lightly on their partners' shoulders.

'Look up at the ceiling, then down to the floor—you can tittle-tattle on anyone moving their shoulders.'

Laughter greeted her suggestion that they tell on each other, and, as it always did, broke up any tension in the room. With brisk efficiency, Nikki led them through what could have been a gym class at school, keeping an eye on those children who had trouble with specific joints, mentally noting who was obviously in pain and might need their medication altered.

She worked in close consultation with Mark to keep them all as pain-free as possible, but in the weeks between visits different joints might become affected, or flares could occur, causing increased swelling.

'They all do the same routine although some are exercising joints that are obviously not affected at all,' David remarked as the children rolled out their gym mats and settled on their backs on the floor.

'In their home routine, they concentrate on their damaged or affected joints,' Nikki told him. 'But here, the ones with injured joints are anxious to match the range of motion of those whose joints aren't affected—makes for good competitiveness. At home, the parents encourage siblings to join the exercises for the same reason. A child with a painful joint will push it so far, and often think that's as far as it goes. Seeing others get more movement makes them try harder.'

'Even when it hurts?'

Nikki frowned at him.

'Especially when it hurts. They live with pain, these kids. They know it like you know—well, your sister, I suppose. They have to treat it, if not as a friend, at least as an acquaintance, and work through it if they possibly can.'

She moved away from him, walking through the supine little bodies as they did leg, arm and shoulder exercises, helping one, encouraging another, talking all the time so the children moved to the rhythm of her voice.

'So, sitting comfortably?' she said, when the thirty minutes she allotted to actual work was up. 'I want to introduce you all to Dr David Campbell, who's here filling in for Dr Mark while he goes to Hollywood where Anna's going to become rich and famous.'

The parents who'd remained for the session all clapped and one of the children yelled hooray. Nikki turned to David.

'Anna not only produces our unit's Christmas pageant, but also coaches the kids in various parts—they're all included—and, as a result, we do the best Christmas show in the hospital.'

'I had noticed you're not averse to dressing up,' he murmured, then he moved away, bending to shake hands with each child in turn, asking names, and chatting quietly.

Nikki waited until he'd introduced himself all around the room then said, 'Well, it's good ideas time. Who's got a good idea today?'

Billy Whatmore, more renowned for mischief than good ideas, shot to his feet.

'Mum's been doing my exercises in the bath. She gets the water real hot and then lets me kick a little plastic ball with my toes. It makes me move my ankle and I don't think about how much it hurts because I laugh a lot at the same time.' He grinned at the other children, then said, 'That's because I make Mum very wet.'

From the back of the room Mrs Whatmore confirmed the downside of this good idea, but Nikki could see that some children would be only too pleased to try out this novel way of exercising.

'I've been doing some of my exercises in bed before I get up,' Kareema Sing offered, in her soft, whispery voice. 'I'm still warm and snugly and Mummy says I'm more 'laxed so it's easier to move my joints.'

Other children chimed in, offering times when they found exercising more enjoyable or practical.

'Now the hair,' Susan reminded Nikki, when the session had ended and most parents were herding children out the door.

'Four braids only,' Nikki told her. 'Two each, otherwise we'll all be here until midnight.'

'You'll keep them in until next session?' Emma asked. 'You promise?'

Nikki sighed. Just what she'd always wanted—four tiny beaded braids clanking around her head for a fortnight. The only bright spot was that David Campbell had left the room, walking out, deep in conversation with one of the few fathers who attended her sessions.

Susan's mother produced the necessary combs, bits of coloured thread and beads, and Nikki sat down with a child on either side of her, succumbing to her fate.

'Here you are. I've been searching everywhere for you. What on earth are you doing now?'

Crystal burst in like a whirlwind, pulling up short when she saw Nikki and her attendants, then grinning like a Cheshire cat.

'What does it look like I'm doing?' Nikki retorted. 'Were you searching everywhere for any reason or just to have a good laugh at my expense?'

'I was careful *not* to laugh,' Crystal told her. 'I know how touchy you can be! I just wanted to check that you'd heard we're having a "goodbye and good luck" drink with Mark in the common room. Five-thirty, so you're already late. Anna's coming in to say goodbye as well.'

Crystal's lips twitched as if striving to hold back another smile, then she turned away and left the room, but not before Nikki saw her shoulders shaking with suppressed mirth and began to wonder just how bad four small braids could end up looking.

Unbelievably awful, that was how bad, she realised a little later when the children produced a mirror so she could admire their handiwork.

'That's wonderful,' she lied, and was rewarded by two beaming smiles, then four small arms going around her neck to reward her with two comprehensive hugs.

Nikki thanked them again, and said goodbye, leaving the mothers to pack up the odds and ends before taking the two girls home. She was heading for the washroom to consider how she might camouflage the braids when David reappeared.

'Oh, that's very nice!' he said, but unlike Crystal he didn't hide his laughter, guffawing in a most unseemly manner.

'Both those girls have arthritic fingers. It's a triumph for them to even try something this fiddly,' she informed him loftily. She intended to sweep on past him, but he reached out and one touch of his hand on her arm brought her to a sudden halt. She explained about her promise to Emma, but

David still asked, 'I realise it's in a good cause, but do you seriously have to wear them until the next session?'

The smile on his face was causing havoc in her body, so much so that she patted the offending plaits uncertainly and muttered, 'I haven't had a good look at them yet, but maybe I can redo them so they're not too awful. I've got to try to keep them in for the kids' sakes.'

'Well, if you're game so am I,' he said, surprising her so much she thought her mouth had probably dropped open. 'I was looking for directions to the common room for this farewell do, but if you'll guide me I can be your escort.'

He reached for her hand and tucked it into the crook of his arm, patted it, as if to keep it in place, then said, 'Which way, oh, braided beauty?'

'Hmmph,' Nikki snorted as she waved her hand towards the corridor they had to follow. 'And you thought I was having a bad hair day earlier!'

She spoke lightly, carrying on with the joke, but it was hard when her toes wanted to dance with excitement at being so close to him, and her heart was pretending this was real, not politeness.

CHAPTER FOUR

IT WAS one thing walking into a small gathering of colleagues with untidy braids clinging to her head, Nikki realised later, but quite another doing it on the arm of a new and gorgeous man. Particularly when 'small' was not the right word.

'The chap who's standing head and shoulders above the rest is my brother, Peter. Crystal's husband,' she said, spying Peter on the opposite side of the room. 'The entire hospital's turned out for this farewell.'

'You don't approve?'

'No, I'm just surprised,' she said. 'I mean, it's not as if he's going for ever. It's leave-of-absence.'

Now she'd had a better look at the crowd, it was predominantly female. Had the grapevine been working overtime? Had the details of Mark's replacement included the fact he was single as well as incredibly handsome?

'I don't know half these people so I'll be no earthly use at introductions and you've met all the unit staff by now.' She unlatched her hand from his arm and stepped ahead of him, but before she could move away he grabbed her shoulder.

'Hey, you can't leave me to fend for myself.' He whispered the words anxiously into her ear. 'Look at all the women!'

Ignoring the tingling sensation his hand was causing on her shoulder, she faced him again.

'You're scared of women? A great hulking brute like you, needing protection from the weaker sex?'

His impressive shoulders moved in a way she'd have

taken to be embarrassment if she didn't know he was so self-assured, walking naked into this room probably wouldn't embarrass him.

Which would be interesting to see...

'I'm not scared.' He broke into the sidetrack her flighty musings had taken. 'And I can't say this without seeming to be full of myself, but women seem to be attracted to me.' He looked directly into her eyes with an expression so earnest she almost believed he was disconcerted by this trend. Almost! 'Most women, that is.'

The addendum seemed to say, everyone but you, which was just fine as far as Nikki was concerned. The last thing she wanted was for him to guess her own body had fallen victim to his abundant physical charms.

'Oh, I can't think why,' she said scathingly, then walked on, not inviting him to accompany her, but not telling him he couldn't either.

She introduced him to staff she did know, ignoring the coy smiles and velvety eyelashes fluttered in his direction. They finally reached Peter, and Nikki decided she'd done enough to protect this wimp from predatory females.

'David Campbell, meet Peter Barclay. He's a cricket fan, Peter, but on the wrong side.'

The introduction worked, the two men soon embroiled in a heated debate over umpiring decisions in the first Test. She edged away, taking a circuitous path towards the door, where Anna and Mark were already farewelling people who had appointments or calls to duty.

'Love the hair!'

So many people made that, or a similar enough remark, Nikki's fingers curled into fists, and it was only will-power and a determination not to start more gossip that prevented her from biffing one of them.

'Good luck,' she said to Anna, giving her a warm hug. 'And make sure Mark does his duty as your consort. No

slacking off to languish by the pool in the company of
sultry starlets, you hear.'

She addressed the last sentence to Mark, then kissed him
on the cheek.

'I hope it's everything you both dreamed it would be,'
she said, taking a hand of each and beaming at them. 'Now,
I'm going to slope off. I haven't shopped properly for a
fortnight, just getting enough to live off from Mrs Lewis
in the mall each evening. It might be keeping her in plastic
aprons but I'll be reduced to eating the floorboards if I don't
refill the pantry on my way home.'

'If you're going shopping, I'd take the dingle dangles
out of your hair,' Anna suggested.

Nikki's hands flew up to touch the offending braids.

'I keep forgetting about them,' she wailed. 'Anna, you're
good with hair—is there anything I can do to make them
less obvious? I have to try to keep them in. It's important
to keep faith with the youngsters.'

'Sit down and I'll have a fiddle,' Anna said, reaching up
and taking hold of one braid. 'There's a chair behind you.'

But there wasn't a chair—not immediately behind her.
There was David Campbell, who once again caught her as
she tipped off balance because she was still tethered to
Anna by the braid. This time, his strong hands supported
her until she felt the chair and could drop down into it.

'I don't know why you keep creeping up on me like
that,' she told him crossly. 'I've bumped into you more
often in the last twenty-four hours than other people in my
entire lifetime.'

'There, there,' Anna said, 'I can't do anything if you
keep moving your head to glare at David.'

'You're not taking them out?' David demanded.

Disobeying Anna, Nikki moved again, to fire another
scowl in his direction.

'No, I'm just tidying them up,' Anna told him. 'Though

why she lets herself in for this kind of thing, I have no idea. Perhaps you'll have more control over her than Mark. Persuade her that there are limits to what she can do for ''her kids'', as she calls them.'

Anna softened the words by patting Nikki's shoulder.

'You're done,' she added. 'I've pinned them back so they look as if they're meant to be lopsided. You might start a new trend.'

Nikki managed to say thank you, but, although she appreciated Anna's attention, her body was in turmoil over David Campbell's continued presence, especially the hand still resting on her shoulder.

To her tormented mind, it was as if he were laying claim to her, but she knew that was impossible. Perhaps he'd forgotten it was there. Maybe he left appendages lying around in much the same way as some people misplaced their glasses.

'Off you go,' Anna said, but the physical Nikki couldn't move, warmed by the hand, happy under its weight, not wanting to lose this contact.

Which is so ridiculous I can't believe you're thinking that way, her inner self derided.

The inner self won, and she stood up, said another goodbye to her friends, then strode away, hoping it didn't look as if she was fleeing, but determined to put some space between herself and David Campbell.

She was almost at the lift when she remembered the folder full of information he'd asked her to peruse, so detoured to her office and collected it, her briefcase, and her car keys.

'I suppose you'd have remembered them when you reached the car park,' she muttered scornfully to herself. 'Really, Nicole, you can't let a man get to you like this.'

She continued to berate herself, but silently, all the way to the car, where her thought processes were once again stalled by his presence. Lounging against his super machine, he gave the impression he was waiting for her.

'What do you want now?' she demanded. 'If it's to talk about your grand plan, then I have to tell you I haven't had a moment to so much as glance at it.'

She bleeped her doors unlocked and was about to open the driver's side when she remembered Emma.

'But I'll definitely look at the papers tonight. If you think it is possible to keep control over the side effects, then little Emma, one of the girls who did my hair, do you think...?'

As usual when she was in this man's company, she was leaping too far ahead, falling over her words when she wasn't falling over her feet.

'I wasn't waiting to talk to you about the papers,' he said. 'I was waiting because Mark said you'd scampered out of the party to do some shopping and my sister phoned me earlier with a list of some things she simply had to have if I wish to eat this evening. I thought you might point me in the right direction as far as supermarkets are concerned.'

Nikki was too affronted by the beginning of his conversation to take much notice of the end.

'I did *not* scamper,' she said, then realised how irrelevant her indignation was. Particularly as this man seemed to think he could go shopping with her. Not that she could forbid him entrance to Sainsbury's, and to refuse to tell him where to go wouldn't do much for international relations.

But shopping with him wouldn't do much for her equilibrium.

And which was more important at the moment?

Equilibrium won hands down, but, unable to think of a believable excuse, she sought refuge in grouchiness.

'You can follow me if you like,' she told him.

He opened the car door and held it for her, his manners making her behaviour seem even more ungracious.

But he's unsettling me, she wailed to herself, hoping to ease the pangs of guilt striking outwards from her conscience.

All the more reason for you to behave, it told her.

In the end, their shopping expedition wasn't as bad as she'd expected. To expedite matters, she asked to see his list, and, apart from having to stand close by him while she read it, she was able to direct him to all the items, and avoid the aisles she knew he'd be using. She then hovered unnecessarily behind the fruit and vegetable displays, knowing his short list should be quickly filled.

Her avoidance tactics meant missing out on a few staples she'd intended to buy, and, for some reason, when she reached the checkout, she had six packets of chocolate biscuits, but she also had enough food to keep her alive for the next week, so—

'Like chocolate biscuits, do you?'

More chocolate, only auditory this time.

'I thought you'd have been long gone by now,' she responded, controlling her galloping heart by concentrating ferociously on the cashier.

'I was seduced by the range of cheeses,' he admitted, making the weak part of her wish she'd had cheese on her list. 'So many to choose from, and cheeses like Cheshire that actually come from Cheshire.'

'It's very bad for your cholesterol,' she told him, trying to avoid seeing the complex images of cheese and David Campbell and seduction her mind managed to conjure up.

'Worse than chocolate biscuits?'

'Boy, can you find a chink in a girl's armour,' she muttered. 'Are you this glib with all women or are you using me for target practice?'

'Actually,' he said, drawling out the word as if he was thinking at the same time, 'I'd prefer us to be seen as friends. Perhaps more than friends. Crystal tells me there's no one special in your life at the moment. Could you spare a month to do a favour for a poor, unattached bloke from down under?'

She must be hallucinating—only wasn't that visual? She was hearing things, hearing voices—a voice—and her mind was scrambling up the words.

'What on earth are you getting at?' she demanded, and saw the smile that so delighted her erring heart flash across his lips.

'It didn't occur to me until we walked into that room this evening. If your hospital is anything like others I've worked in, then word has already gone out that I'm single. I know it sounds vain and pretentious when I put it into words, but women do seem to be attracted to me, and right now I don't need any more complications in my life. If you could pretend—just go along with a small deception— make it look as if we might have something going, well, it would provide protective colouring for me, if you see what I mean.'

'He obviously regards you as immune to his charms,' the checkout girl said helpfully. 'Mind you, if he made the offer to me, I'd jump at it. Think how much your own reputation will gain, being seen with such a good-looking man.'

Nikki shook her head to clear it of the nonsensical voices, then turned to face the man behind her, oblivious to the queue gathering behind them.

'And what exactly do you want me to do to give this impression of a love-struck swain? Run panting after you down the hospital corridors? Smile coyly up at you when I'm in the middle of a therapy session? Why should I care if every single woman, and any of the married ones as well, for that matter, chase after you?'

She had her gaze fixed on his tie in order to avoid looking into his eyes, so caught the movement of his chest as he breathed in, then slowly released the breath.

'It would give me more time to do real work because there'd be fewer interruptions. If we can reach some conclusions from our debates then maybe early treatment for Emma might be possible.'

Her head jerked upwards as she realised this was no time for avoidance tactics.

'That's blackmail,' she said, wondering if her eyes conveyed the storminess of her feelings.

He smiled and nodded.

'Yes, it is,' he agreed, then he touched her on the shoulder. 'Now, don't you think we've held up this queue for long enough?'

She spun away, paid for her groceries, then shoved the trolley viciously towards the door, wishing he were in front of her, not behind, so she could ram it into his legs.

Accidentally, of course.

'And you wouldn't have to pant after me down corridors. I've never been one for extreme shows of emotion. Just the occasional lunch should do the trick.' He'd caught up and was pushing his trolley along beside hers in a companionable way. 'And perhaps walking out to our cars together, or into hospital functions. Would it be such an imposition? After all, didn't Mark ask you to take care of me? Weren't those his last words as you scampered out of the drinks party?'

She couldn't argue over his terminology again, nor could she deny Mark saying something of the kind.

'But you don't even like me,' she bleated, the words sounding so pathetic she felt herself blushing.

'Nonsense,' he said. 'I might think you're a bit dippy, the way you go about things, but apparently you get results, and I won't argue with that.'

'Scampering' and now 'a bit dippy'. She shook her head again, but that didn't seem to help.

'I'll think about it,' she told him, stopping behind her car and facing him again, seeing the way his blue eyes seemed to lighten when he smiled. 'Though why a man of your age and size and obvious experience should need someone to run interference for him, I don't know. You must have been turning away unwanted females for years, pushing them back in droves. By now, you should have perfected the technique.'

Now the eyes darkened again and she felt a twinge of compunction for speaking so flippantly.

'I married very young,' he said. 'That provides its own protection. While it lasts.'

This time he didn't open her car door, but pushed his trolley across the car park to where the big Range Rover stood, gleaming softly beneath a yellow spotlight.

Well, she'd asked for it. Or she supposed she had. Now she was going to be tormented by all the questions that provoked. What happened in his marriage? Did his wife die? Or was he divorced? Was that why his sister's divorce had left him bitter?

Could she ask him?

She doubted it. Even for a pretend love-interest with no reserve or reticence, it would be prying.

She opened the boot and dumped her shopping bags inside, then slammed it shut and pushed the trolley back towards the building.

The black Range Rover was gone, driven out while she was asking unanswerable questions, she guessed, but the image of its driver as he'd been when she'd entered the car park at work, slouched elegantly against the big vehicle, remained with her as she drove home.

It stuck around as she unpacked, and ate her dinner, staying long enough to haunt her dreams and disturb her sleep, so she rose, tired, cranky, and bleary-eyed the next morning.

She'd put a stop to his nonsense, she'd decided, in the wee hours of the morning. Tell him it wasn't on.

Buoyed by this resolve, she poured herself a glass of juice, fixed a bowl of healthy cereal, then sat down to re-read his facts and figures on the use of more aggressive treatment in the early stages of JRA.

It made even more sense than it had the previous evening, when some of it had struck her as brilliant. The thought brought with it a little niggle of uncertainty.

Well, she could agree with him professionally without playing the besotted lover.

She rinsed her breakfast dishes and left them on the sink, checked the braids were still pinned back in an approximation of the way Anna had fixed them, then headed off for work again, telling herself that wearing a little make-up wasn't a sign of weakness, but more like armour to strengthen her resolve. Now all she had to do was keep out of his way as much as possible.

She couldn't see his car anywhere so she hopped out of hers with confidence, and strode towards the lift.

'Good morning!'

His cheery greeting made her jump at least six inches and she turned on him, all but spitting with rage.

'What are you doing lurking around like that?' she demanded. 'Scaring people out of their wits?'

He turned his head and glanced around.

'I can't see any people,' he said blandly. 'Only you, and I was waiting for you. I'm sorry if I startled you, but perhaps it's a good sign. Perhaps you were deep in thought, rehearsing the little sidelong glances you might give me should the opportunity arise.'

'In your dreams, buster!' Nikki told him. 'The only sidelong glances I'll be giving you is when I'm wondering about your sanity. And even if I was willing to go along with your mad scheme, when do you think I'd have time for sidelong glances? You may consider this filling-in job a doddle, but I work here, you know. All day every day. There's rarely time to scratch myself, let alone cast sidelong glances.'

The lift arrived and he moved closer to her as they stepped inside.

'Perhaps I could do your scratching, would that save you some time?'

His voice was so low and husky, it seemed to rasp across her skin, making it itchy all over—needing to be scratched.

'I like the idea of the panel to discuss treatments and I've some names of people you might contact. I think you should include a physician, so any discussion on possible long-term effects can be guided by an expert beyond our field.'

'Avoiding an answer, Nikki?' Now the words were teasing, but no more so than the closeness of his body.

'Talking shop, which is all the talk there'll be between us,' she said gruffly, wishing the doors would open and set her free.

She reached into her briefcase and found his file. 'The names are in there, Claire will get you the contact numbers.'

She thrust it at him as the doors finally slid apart, then walked quickly away. Remembered his comments about scampering, and slowed down, hoping to give the impression of a glide more than a scamper.

Her plan to keep out of his way, although it had foundered slightly to begin with, worked well up to lunch-time, when she decided to avoid both the canteen and the coffee shop and cravenly headed for Dunwoody, the little shop where Mrs Lewis held sway. She'd buy some fruit and perhaps a health bar, and take a walk in the park.

*   *   *

'It's unbelievable that there's so much green space in a city the size of London. And to be working so close to Regent's Park, a place I've heard of for years. It's mind boggling, that's what it is.'

He fell into step beside her before she'd gone a hundred yards, holding an identical bag from Dunwoody.

'Are you following me?' she asked, and didn't believe for a moment the innocent expression on his face.

'Quite the opposite. I was standing under that tree wondering which path to take when you came along. I must say, my heart gave a leap of gladness, thinking perhaps you'd changed your mind and decided to help me out with this protective business.'

'Well, I haven't,' Nikki told him, 'so you can forget leaping hearts and gladness. But if you can talk and walk and eat, I'd like to talk to you about immunosuppressive drugs like methotrexate. Mark's been using that lately to treat the children you'd be considering for your aggressive treatment. And it's been in use in larger doses for treating cancer in children without too many ill effects. Isn't that a safer way to go?'

He seemed to accept the conversational switch with easy grace.

'We've been using it too, and have had good results, but it isn't a cure. It seems to work by slowing down cell proliferation so decreasing swelling and improving the physical symptoms, but it doesn't cure the disease and children have to keep taking it—some of them for as long as ten or fifteen years. When you consider it has unpleasant side effects while the child is on it—mouth sores, stomach upset, lung and liver inflammation—the long-term use of it is uncomfortable, to say the least.'

Nikki moved easily to his pace and found herself enjoying the medical debate, thinking how much she might have liked his company, enjoyed playing up to him, if her foolish heart hadn't been struck all of a heap the first—or was it the second?—time she'd seen him.

'Do you stop to eat? Should we find a seat?'

His questions took her by surprise, but she managed to nod a yes to both of them, then followed him to a shady, and unexpectedly unoccupied, seat overlooking the canal.

She sank down on it, and leaned back, closing her eyes as she stretched her neck and wiggled her shoulders to release the tension his presence unwittingly generated.

'Beautiful,' he murmured, and her eyelids flew upward to catch him looking directly at her.

'What is?'

'Why, the park, the ambience. London itself, I suppose. This whole experience is very special to me.'

The words sounded genuine enough but he didn't look around at the park or the ambience, or even what could be seen of London. He kept looking at her, at her eyes, his gaze skimming across her face, hesitating on her lips then back to her eyes so she was again drawn into the blueness and sent spinning into a frenzy by the sensation.

'Eat your lunch,' she told him. 'And tell me why the even more damaging side effects of corticosteroids—prednisone, I imagine you're considering—would be more acceptable than those of methotrexate.'

He opened his paper bag and peered inside, finally extracting a health bar identical to the one she'd chosen.

'Do you think that's a portent of some kind?' he asked, holding it up beside hers, and accidentally brushing her fingers.

'Considering Mrs Lewis only has three varieties, it's more like a mathematical probability.'

Nikki tucked her fingers out of harm's reach and waited for him to stop trying to divert her and answer the question. He didn't know she'd had to ask it, not wholly because of interest in the subject, but as a diversion of her own. Shop talk was infinitely easier to handle than personal revelations and friendly banter.

He must have felt the same way, for, without further prompting, he continued to talk about his idea. Through lunch, then as they walked back along the path, and on into the main entrance of the hospital.

'It reminds me of pictures of old railway stations,' he remarked as they entered the elegant, glassed-in area, flanked by little shops to make a kind of mini-mall.

Nikki looked around, seeing surroundings she'd been taking for granted.

'Or the hot houses at Kew,' she said.

'I haven't been to Kew,' David remarked, taking her arm to steer her around a family group who'd stopped in the middle of the entry to stage a voluble domestic dispute.

'I go there often. I love the trees and gardens, but especially the glasshouses.'

The enthusiasm she felt for the lovely park must have dulled her instinct, so when he said, 'I don't suppose you'd care to show me around some time?' she was left floundering.

'M-maybe,' she stammered. 'Some time.'

'This weekend?' he said hopefully. 'Sunday?'

'No, no, I'm busy Sunday,' she managed, wondering what on earth she could do on Sunday so it wouldn't be a lie. She *was* going to Peter and Crystal's for dinner, but that was hardly relevant to daytime busyness.

'Well, another Sunday, then,' he said, apparently unperturbed by her refusal.

Blue eyes gleamed into hers with so much delight she couldn't bring herself to deny him the possibility, but deep inside her warning bells were clanging. Yesterday, David Campbell had been abrupt to the point of rudeness. He'd sniped at her and challenged her and poked and probed, showing no sign that he saw her as anything other than a colleague, and not a very important one at that.

Today, he was using his not inconsiderable charm. Why? To bamboozle her into providing his camouflage for the month?

It didn't gel.

CHAPTER FIVE

THE answer to Nikki's unasked question came later, as she was preparing to leave work with a pile of files tucked under her right arm, her briefcase in her hand, and two long foam rubber poles only partially balanced under the left arm.

'Are you hoping to get into the lift with all that gear? Perhaps I could take your weapons.'

It had to be David who'd caught her although it was well after six and she'd assumed he'd be long gone. Not that she'd been hiding in her office!

'They're not mine. I borrowed them from my younger brother and he'll want them back.' She let him rescue them, and stalwartly ignored the sensations twitching at her skin when his hands brushed it in the transfer. 'I thought they might be fun in the pool but they're actually too long for any of the children I treat.'

She explained this quite rationally, she thought, as he ushered her into the lift.

'I'm surprised you didn't cut them in half,' he murmured, smiling and nodding at the other occupants of the lift, and holding the poles as if he walked around with six-foot lengths of dense foam rubber all the time.

'I would have, but they belong to Gerald's water polo team and I thought the members might be cross,' she said, then caught the gleam of humour in his eyes and realised he'd been teasing.

'Well, they've possibilities,' she told him, leading the way into the car park. 'These are too thick. I'm going to approach a manufacturer about getting thinner and shorter versions so children can grip them. Wielding them in the pool will provide great shoulder and arm exercise, and bashing other people should release frustration and aggression so the kids would get a psychological workout as well!'

'Does your mind never stop working on ways to provide activities for your patients? Don't you ever switch off?'

She opened the rear door of her car.

'Of course I switch off,' she asserted, then caught his eyebrows lifting as she shifted the pile of files from one arm to the other so she could put them on the back seat. 'They're old files I wanted to read through—for your wretched project, if you must know. I thought I might find another ex-patient to include on your panel.'

He moved closer to her, sending her body into a tingle of delight as he shoved the reluctant poles into the car then shut the door on them.

'I'm sorry to be giving you extra work,' he said as he straightened—not looking at all sorry, now she could see his face. 'If you were intending looking at them tonight, why not stop off at my place and we could go through them together? Halve the work. Perhaps have a drink at the same time. I'd like you to meet my sister.' He paused, then added, 'And my niece.'

Nikki had been about to refuse, to tell him she'd seen through his ploy and knew he was pursuing his ridiculous idea of pretending there was something between them, but his voice had changed as he'd added the last sentence, something in the intonation catching in her mind and triggering curiosity.

'I suppose I could,' she said, her original reluctance shading her voice.

'You shouldn't pretend so hard to be overjoyed by the suggestion,' David told her, smiling in a way that made heat pool low down in her body.

'As it's your panel, I suppose the suggestion makes sense,' she said tartly. 'I'll see you there.'

She climbed in behind the wheel and fired the engine as he shut the door for her. Couldn't fault his manners—they were impeccable. Then why was she so reluctant to spend more time with him? Wouldn't seeing more of him be helpful? Kind of like an immunisation for love where, by exposing herself to the cause, she would eventually develop resistance?

The theory was one thing, but in fact...

She drove towards the quiet square, wondering what his sister was like—and what she'd make of her brother bringing home a 'strapping wench' with four untidy braids in her hair.

Not much, if Meg Lindsay's cool greeting was any indication. Her 'how do you do?' was perfunctory, and the top-to-toe visual scan she afforded Nikki was dismissive. Meg's black hair was swept into a chignon, and the blue eyes looked more like ice-chips than Mediterranean skies, but the family resemblance was marked.

'You did promise Jasmine you'd play Monopoly with her tonight.' She addressed the words to David but contrived to make Nikki feel even more uncomfortable.

'Why she wants to play Monopoly when she should be visiting all the places on the board is beyond me,' David replied, and once again Nikki detected something in his voice. It went beyond the irritation he was trying to hide from his sister—almost to a kind of sadness.

Or was she imagining things? Her mind reading too much into the vocal nuances of a virtual stranger?

Meg excused herself and walked off, every step of her retreat proclaiming a silent disapproval.

'Meg and I are at odds over Jazzy,' David offered by way of explanation, then he waved Nikki towards a room on the right of the front foyer—a comfortable, book-lined study, she discovered. 'Very much at odds.'

'What a great room.' The praise was automatic, for the room not only looked comfortable but exuded a feeling of ease. It also provided a handy switch in conversation as Nikki knew she didn't want to be drawn into his family's dynamics. 'You mentioned ambience earlier—this kind of room epitomises it for me.'

'A book-lined study in dull tones of maroon and grey. I thought you'd go for something—'

'Gaudier?' Nikki demanded, then glanced down at the smock she'd worn to work today—a comfortable denim shirt with bright balloons appliqued all over it. She raised her hands in surrender.

He grinned and waved her to a high-backed leather armchair.

'Would you accept a drink as a peace-offering?'

'A gin and tonic without the gin, please,' she replied as the smile sent her heart into new spasms and made her realise that alcohol and attraction could be a too-potent cocktail for her to handle.

So much for immunisation.

While he poured the drinks, Nikki spread the files on the desk, sorting them into two piles.

'Half each,' she said, raising her glass in a salute. 'I've given you the ones I think more likely to interest you. One young woman there, Cecilia Cooper, has been a spokesperson for paediatric arthritis sufferers since she was twelve when she decided SLE wasn't going to stop her having a life.'

'Systemic Lupus Erythematosus. Poor kid. Was it serious involvement?'

'Serious enough for her to be treated with the steroids you're advocating—prednisone. She was also on the anti-malarial drug for a long time, and ended up with permanent damage to her hips, but so far no signs of damage to her kidneys. None of it has stopped her headlong rush through life. At present she's at the London School of Economics and informally engaged to another of my brothers, Andrew, the middle one, nearest to me in age and probably temperament. He didn't get reserve or reticent either. He's an agent for rock groups.'

'An agent for rock groups?'

Nikki glanced up from the file she'd been scanning to meet bemused blue eyes.

'You know, does the bookings for them, that kind of thing.'

From the look on David's face, her explanation didn't help much.

'I do know what agents do,' he said. 'It just seems a surprising profession.'

'Unusual perhaps, but, as Andrew is always telling my parents, someone has to do it. And as he makes probably five times as much as the eminent surgeon of the family—and ten times as much as poor old Dad who's a GP—there's not much they can say. He even counters their arguments that it's a family tradition to work in service to others by saying he's doing that for all the hundreds of thousands of people who flock to his bands' concerts.'

'And did he meet Cecilia through you?'

'Only in a very roundabout way.'

A movement of his arched eyebrows asked the next question.

'I did suggest she phone him to see if he knew of any new bands who might be willing to do a charity gig for the publicity—as against real money. She must have worked some special wiles on him, because he ended up organising the whole show, and she ended up a fixture in his life. Now, shouldn't we be working?'

She took a sip of tonic and pulled another file towards

her. Chatting to David Campbell was all very well, but it
was giving her body false notions about her purpose in
stopping off at his place—and not doing much for the immune process.

'You're very close to your brothers, all your family?'

The question startled her and she raised her head again.

'Of course I am. We're all close—good friends, really,
now we're over all the squabbling and sibling rivalry stuff.
But it must be the same in your family for you and your
sister to be travelling together.'

'That's a very broad assumption,' he replied, then he
pulled a file towards him and began reading, dropping the
personal conversation as suddenly as he'd begun it.

Or had she begun it, then he'd carried it on?

Whatever, they were back to work again now—on safer
ground.

They read through the files, Nikki passing over one more
she thought might interest David. She had decided the rest
were unlikely to prove helpful and was about to suggest
she depart when the soft swishing sound of wheels on carpet made her turn.

It had to be the niece—Jasmine—for her hair was as dark
as her mother's and uncle's, flowing down around her
shoulders in heavy ebony waves, but what stole Nikki's
breath wasn't the wheelchair—a manual one, but obviously
customised in a brilliant royal blue enamel—but the sheer
beauty of the young girl who sat in it.

'Mum says you've got five minutes to dinner, Uncle
David,' the vision said, ignoring Nikki altogether.

David looked up, frowned ferociously, and introduced
his guest.

'We're done here,' Nikki said easily, speaking to
Jasmine before turning to David and adding, 'I checked
before I left work. The phone numbers on those files are

all current. I assume you'll want to contact the people yourself.'

She stood up and he rose at the same time, putting out a hand towards her, then dropping it abruptly.

'You don't have to go. I'm sure Meg's dinner will stretch to feed one more.'

'You promised, Uncle David.'

The unmistakable threat in the young girl's voice made Nikki turn in amazement that someone would speak to an adult so rudely. She caught a flush of anger in the girl's cheeks and a petulant droop to the lovely mouth.

And knew she would be caught in the crossfire if she stayed a moment longer.

'I really must go,' she said, turning back to David, 'although it's kind of you to offer to feed me.'

His eyes were grave. No doubt he was saddened by his niece's behaviour, and suddenly Nikki wanted to see him smile again.

She put out her hand to shake his in goodbye and said, 'I could probably show you around Kew the following Sunday.'

He took her hand and shook it, then let her take it back, not holding it a moment longer than was necessary. And although his lips smiled, his eyes didn't, remaining sombre and distressed, looking not at Nikki but beyond her to his niece.

Then he seemed to pull himself together and he gave Nikki a better smile.

'I've got five minutes, I'll walk you to your car,' he said. 'Tell your mother I'll be right back,' he added to Jasmine.

He took Nikki's arm and walked her to the door, saying nothing until they were outside.

'Okay, Miss Barclay, you seem to like a challenge. You won't take on the protective role for me, but would you accept another one?'

She edged away so she could look into his face.

'What is it?' she asked, thrown off balance by the fact he still looked sombre and depressed.

'Jasmine.'

The word hung in the twilit air for a second before Nikki repeated it.

'It's a long story and I haven't time to tell it now,' he said. 'I know you're busy on Sunday but would you have an hour to spare some time tomorrow? Could I call at your place or meet you somewhere, explain the problems we've been having with Jasmine? Even if you don't feel up to helping her, you might have some advice you could give me.'

'What's caused her disability?' Nikki asked, disturbed by the change in David's mood.

'You want one guess?' David said, and once again his lips smiled but his eyes didn't. 'I'll save you the bother. It's JRA, polyarticular.'

Nikki shook her head as she dealt with shock, and the surge of sympathy he wouldn't want to hear.

'It must be bad for her to be confined to a wheelchair.'

'You'd think so,' he said, his voice gravelly, the chocolate full of razor-blades again. 'Are you willing to help? Even listen and advise? Will I come to you or shall we meet? I'd be happy to buy you coffee, a beer, lunch, whatever would suit you.'

This was another David—a man who sounded almost desperate.

A man who loved his niece very much, Nikki guessed.

'Come to my place. Early if you like—that way you'll still have the day free to spend with your sister. It's easier to talk in private than in a pub or café.' She fished in the pocket of her jeans and pulled out her car keys, twisted open the slim card-case attached to the keyring, and handed him a slightly dog-eared card. 'I always carry a few, but I rarely get asked for them. I don't meet many prospective customers on the street. My flat's on the ground floor.'

She spoke lightly to hide the emotion she was feeling. Pity would be the last thing David Campbell would accept from her or anyone else.

'How early? Six o'clock?' he teased, and she was pleased to see he'd relaxed again.

'Only if you want to run with me, but I should warn you that, although being able to chat while running is a good indication that you're travelling at a sensible pace, it's not something I've ever mastered. I manage a breathless "good morning" to a few dog-walkers I meet along the way, but that's the best I can do. I'm always home by seven-thirty, then sweat-free and ready for a light breakfast by eight. Would eight suit you?'

He nodded, then took her hand.

'Thank you,' he said, grave again now, but the touch renewed the now-familiar tremors in her skin, and his eyes were no less potent because they didn't smile.

Nikki drove home, thinking of all the questions she should have asked, working out possible diagnoses from the brief glimpse she'd had of the sulky child.

In the end, she decided it was useless speculation and allowed herself an end-of-week treat, picking up a Chinese take-away as a first indulgence, then allowing herself to brood over how good David Campbell looked in the book-lined study as a second.

Not a good idea, as he again lingered on in her thoughts, and sneaked into her dreams.

Which meant a late start to her run, minimum stretching before she set out, and a dreadful cramp that left her hobbling the last mile home.

Naturally, given the fates she had against her, he was already at her place when she struggled up the drive to the old detached house, set well back from the road in its tree-studded ground.

He'd been sitting in his car, the driver's door open, and a morning paper spread across the wheel.

'Sprained something?' he asked, climbing down and hurrying to assist her. He stretched a strong arm around her back, and held her close to support her.

'No, it's just a cramp and it's going, but in the meantime the stuff I'm shedding all over your clothes isn't distilled water.'

He grinned at her.

'I've never been one to let a little sweat bother me. Anyway, I understood sweat was a male prerogative, while women went for perhaps a little dewy perspiration.'

She edged away but found his banter comforting—and fun!

'Well, I've dewed enough on you and I really am okay. Would you mind shifting your car around to the left side of the house? There's a parking space for visitors. It says "Flat One". I'll open the door on that side so you can come straight in while I have a shower.'

Once again her reactions to the man were making her dithery. And once again she had to remind herself that past experience had proved her body was a most unreliable measure of a man's suitability. Not that this man had shown the slightest interest in her—not in that way.

And why should he? she wondered, gloomily facing her reflection in the bathroom mirror. First a clown, then a shiny-faced mess, followed by the braid business, while today she looked like an accident that had happened to someone else.

She stripped off her trainers, and her damp jogging clothes, casting them all into a smelly heap in the corner of the room. She'd deal with them later. She showered, then realised she hadn't brought clean clothes into the bathroom—that she never brought clean clothes into the bathroom because her bedroom was a step away across the hall and there was never anyone around to be offended by her nudity as she took that step.

Wrapping a too-small towel ineffectively around her body, she leapt across the intervening space, ignoring the twinge in her cramped calf and praying her visitor would be immersed in his paper once again.

He said nothing when she emerged in jeans and a cotton sweater, not many minutes later.

'Shouldn't you have stretched after your run?' he asked, glancing up from the paper as she walked into the living room and giving no indication he'd seen her flash across the hall.

'I was too sore to stretch,' she told him, wondering why he should be concerned about her physical well-being. Breakfast was a safer subject. She moved so the kitchen divider was between them. 'I've juice and cereal, bread if you'd like toast, coffee or tea.'

'A cup of coffee, thanks. I've done breakfast already.'

Thinking hunger might be exacerbating her reactions to him, she put on the kettle, popped bread into the toaster and poured herself a glass of grape juice.

The kitchen was a converted corner of what had been a long drawing room in the original house, so she could see her guest as she pottered around, acutely uncomfortable in her own domain.

'Is Jasmine's JRA sero-positive?' she asked, starting the conversational ball rolling to let her body know this was business not pleasure, and that she had no intention of giving in to its weakness.

'Why would you think that when it's only found in such a small percentage of JRA sufferers—something like five per cent?'

Seems like he was back to the aggressive David who'd questioned her clown therapy!

'Because of the wheelchair, I guess. Most patients with polyarticular JRA, particularly the sero-negative ones, have involvement in the small joints, toes, wrists, fingers. I've only had one patient who was sero-positive and even she responded to treatment and was left relatively free of any after-effects.'

The toast popped up and she spread it with marmalade, made coffee for herself and David, assuming black with no sugar was his usual way of taking it. Then, unable to think of a reason to delay any further, she set it all on a tray and carried it through to the small coffee-table in the living room.

She indicated his coffee with a wave of her hand, then picked up a square of toast and settled into the armchair opposite him, ready to enjoy her breakfast—or to pretend to enjoy it so he wouldn't hone in on her uneasiness at his presence in her living room.

'She's sero-negative, developed the first symptoms at three—'

'How old is she now? Is her illness what prompted you to specialise in rheumatology?'

He sipped his coffee then smiled grimly at her across the rim of the cup.

'Yes, to the last question, for all the good it's done Jazzy!' he said, then he shrugged, as if to remove a burden from his shoulders and continued. 'She didn't ever seem badly affected; a little anaemic, fussy about her food, thin for her age—she's fourteen, by the way.'

'Fourteen!' Surprise forced the word out. Nikki had taken her for a child of ten or eleven.

'Children with polyarticular JRA are usually small for their age, and thin.' He spoke stiffly, defensive of any implied criticism of his niece.

'Yes, I remember that, but why the wheelchair? It's the very worst option for any arthritis sufferer, to take to wheels. You must know that. They lose their muscle tone and strength, and their range of motion and eventually, if their legs are bent all day, they get contractures and end up with legs locked in that position. Have you considered hip replacements if she's in pain , or new knee joints perhaps? Anything to get her mobile again.'

The smile returned, less grim this time. Definitely more appealing.

'I was kind of hoping you might be the "anything".'

Nikki pulled her wits together, berating herself for being sidetracked by a smile.

'Anything?'

'The "anything" that gets her out of the wheelchair,' he replied, then he set down his coffee-cup, leaned back in the chair, and sighed.

'I came to London primarily to meet Mark—and hope-fully spend time working with him, although that's now been stymied. Meg's been gloomy and depressed since her divorce and I think Jazzy must have been badly affected by it as well, because she's changed almost overnight from a bright, happy kid who was dealing well with the arthritis into an impossible, rude, ungracious, demanding, selfish and self-centred, know-all brat.'

Nikki grinned at the description which tallied quite well with what her mother had called her at a similar age.

'I think it's more likely to do with her being a teenager than the arthritis or the divorce, although both could have intensified the symptoms.'

He looked so aghast, she chuckled.

'You *must* have thought of that,' she said. 'Your sister would realise it's an adolescent phase that's fairly normal at her age.'

Another sigh.

'Meg's feeling so sorry for herself I'd doubt she'd notice if Jazzy grew two heads. And because she's so into self-pity, she's taken the easy way out and anything Jazzy wants she can have.'

'Like an electric-blue wheelchair she doesn't really need? How bad is her arthritis? What joints are affected? Is she still suffering flares or is she in remission?'

'I've got her full medical reports with me. I left them in the car because I wasn't certain you'd be willing to help. She certainly has some joint erosion in the ankles and in her knees. She was put on methotrexate early on when it became obvious there were problems. She hasn't had a flare for three years and could possibly be said to be over it, considering her age—'

'But?' Nikki prompted. She was pleased to become involved in his problem, as concentration on it distracted her mind from the carryings on of her body.

'She was left with an ungainly gait, more a roll than a limp. Hence the wheelchair.'

'Good grief, you can't allow that!' Nikki exploded from her chair and flung her arms into the air for good measure. He could hardly miss her disgust. 'Haven't you told her, told her mother, what will happen? Even if she is in permanent remission from the disease, her muscles will become weaker and her knee and ankle joints stiffer. If there are internal scars and permanent bone deterioration, then she probably does suffer some pain when she walks, but putting up with pain is surely a better option than spending her entire life dependent on someone else, which is what will happen if she stays in the wheelchair.'

She paced the room as she spoke, her indignation not allowing her to sit still.

Then she caught the smile on David's face and stopped abruptly.

'You've trapped me into this, haven't you?' she said.

'Even that nonsense about needing protection from women was a lead-up to involving me with your niece. You figured I'd turn you down on that one, but might feel guilty enough to agree to the second part of a double play. But why me? There are a million physios in the world who could probably help Jasmine.'

'Mark said you were the best,' David admitted, not smiling now she'd caught on to his game plan. 'I must say I had doubts when I first met you. I couldn't see Jazzy taking kindly to a clown, but after watching your interaction with patients I'm willing to go along with his judgement.'

'Don't overdo the enthusiasm,' Nikki growled, stalled in her pacing by this unexpected admission. 'And what exactly do you expect me to do? Say, "take up your wheelchair and walk" to Jasmine and expect her to follow? I can see that happening! Especially as we didn't exactly get off on the right foot, or wheel, or whatever, with you carting me along to your place when she was obviously expecting to have you on her own.'

'She has to learn she can't have everything she wants when she wants it,' David said.

Don't we all, Nikki muttered to herself. Some things we can't have, full stop!

'Yes, but that doesn't alter the fact that it wasn't a good start. Have you told her I'm a physio? That you want to involve me in her rehabilitation?'

He looked embarrassed—or as embarrassed as such a confident man could look.

'Well, no,' he admitted slowly. 'I wasn't actually going to mention that part of things, just kind of introduce you into the house as a friend and see if you could weave a bit of magic from that point.'

Flabbergasted didn't begin to describe how she felt! Then anger began to build, slowly at first, but working up towards a good seethe.

'Hence the nonsense you carried on with at the hospital! And how's your sister going to handle this? She didn't exactly fall over herself to welcome me as your colleague— I doubt she'll be rolling out the red carpet if you bring me home as a friend.'

He waved his hand as if to dismiss her objections.

'Meg's a little touchy about females in my life. She's keen to marry me off to this friend of hers, Lucille Morgan. It's been a plan of hers for years.'

Nikki took a minute to steady her breathing, sent into hyperventilation by this bland announcement.

'You sound overjoyed about that arrangement,' she said when her lungs were working properly again. 'Really besottedly in love.'

The sarcasm must have penetrated for he glanced at her in surprise.

'I didn't say I was going along with Meg's plans, but they're worth considering,' he pointed out. 'I've always thought I'd remarry some time, and Lucille's a nice enough woman. It would be practical. We've friends in common, enjoy the same things. I think, as you get older, besotted is probably a mistake, don't you?'

This can't be happening, Nikki thought. I've fallen in love with a man who feels exactly the way I thought I should feel about marriage, only I'm besotted and he doesn't want besotted. Not to mention that he's more or less fixed up.

'No!' She hadn't intended to deny passionate attraction, but her inner self must have felt strongly enough about it to overcome her scruples. 'I don't think age precludes the odd lapse into besottedness, but we're straying rather far from the point here. Will your niece take more notice of me as a presumed friend of yours than she would of me the therapist?'

He hesitated, as if sorting through what she'd said to get to the part that was important to him.

'When I asked her and Meg to come with me to the UK, I spoke of the specialist unit at Lizzie's and I thought she was happy to at least have a look at Lizzie's JRA programmes and perhaps even consider joint replacement for her knees. However, since we arrived, arthritis has become a dirty word, and madam has installed herself permanently in the wheelchair and refuses to move.'

Nikki found herself feeling sorry for the child—struggling not only with adolescence but with being 'different'. But sympathy wouldn't get her out of the chair.

'Does the house have a lift? I presume the bedrooms are on upper levels.'

'There's no lift. We brought the wheelchair with us so she could use it if we went sightseeing. We knew there'd be places where a lot of walking was involved. As I've refused to carry either it or her up the stairs, she does get some exercise going up to and down from her bedroom, but the moans of pain must make the neighbours think we're indulging in medieval torture, and my sister's opinion of my cruelty is voiced every time Jazzy tackles the climb.'

'So your sister's fallen for the "poor little me" act as well? Does she know you're trying to enlist my help in sorting out the problem or will she be against my involvement?'

David stood up, stretched, then carried his cup into the kitchen and rinsed it under the tap.

'I think, deep down, she acknowledges it's wrong for Jazzy to spend all her time in the chair, but she's been through a lot of stress herself and, right now, it's easier for her if I'm seen as the cruel tyrant in the little drama.'

Nikki followed him, running through the scenario in her head.

'It's probably better if Jasmine feels her mother is on her

side,' she agreed, then felt his bulk as he stepped back and she stepped forward, so once again they collided, not heavily, but solidly enough to trigger all the squishy stuff inside her.

Then he bent his head and kissed her softly on the cheek.

She jumped back as if he'd stung her, pressing her back against the divider.

'Sorry, that was gratitude overwhelming me,' he said softly. 'And a thank-you, because you sound as if the problem has you hooked. I know I can't expect miracles, but if you could come up with any idea I'm willing to help put it into practice.'

'I haven't said I'd help,' she bleated, but she knew she would.

He was so close she could smell his shaving cream—a clean smell, not overwhelmed by spice or lemon. And suddenly, the thought of having him for a friend, even a pretend friend, was very enticing. If she could handle all the physical flip-flops inside her—keep them damped down—it might be fun getting to know this man.

CHAPTER SIX

NIKKI was too close to him, her mind distracted by the kiss, which meant nothing, her body revelling in what it seemed to think was her acquiescence in its bad behaviour. Stepping backwards to escape the clean smell, she pretended composure.

'I suppose if we're going to do a "friends" thing, I could get out of what I'm doing and take you to Kew tomorrow. All of you. The wheelchair would be a valid means of getting around in such a large area so I could get to know Jasmine without beginning our relationship with an argument.'

David smiled, the blue eyes gleaming with pleasure, his lips curving seductively.

'I'd kiss you again if you hadn't reacted so violently the first time,' he murmured, his eyes focussing on her lips—not her cheek—as if he was imagining the act.

'A simple thank you will do,' she said primly, but knew a different reaction was visible in the colour blooming in her cheeks. 'Would your sister be interested in Kew? Maybe it's too dull an outing for Jasmine?'

'Meg's mad about gardens. I think they'll both enjoy it,' David promised. 'Especially if I order a very expensive picnic hamper from some shop Meg's been going on about since we arrived. It seems her idea of a trip to England, apart from taking up residence in Harrods, and eating strawberries and cream at Wimbledon, is tartan rugs and wicker picnic hampers on grassy lawns. I think she'd have preferred a Rolls Royce to the Range Rover, but I quibbled over the rental costs.'

Nikki chuckled at this depiction of his sister, and was about to agree that tartan rugs and picnic hampers were the stuff of dreams for her too. Then she remembered the reason for this outing.

'And Jasmine? What were her expectations of the trip?'

David grinned at her.

'From the conversations we had on the long, long flight, I gather she thought living next door to someone called Scary Spice would be cool, although, she assured me, she's too old for the Spice Girls now. She did mention some group who goes for grunge. Is grunge an English word? One familiar to you?'

He's nice as well as devastatingly sexy, Nikki thought, unaccountably moved by his words. And he obviously cares very deeply about his niece to have remembered the teenager's conversation.

She returned his smile with one of her own.

'All Saints!'

'All Saints?'

'I imagine that's the band she was talking about. They dress very badly but they can sing. Now, there's a thought.'

She wandered back into the living room, David temporarily blotted from her mind as she tried to remember where the All Saints' T-shirt bestowed on her by Andrew might be. In the pile of sweaty clothes in the corner of the bathroom. That was where it was. She'd pulled it out of the drawer last night while she was looking for a longer one to wear to bed, and left it out to wear on her run this morning.

'Well, if that's all settled, I've got to go to the laundrette, and you've got a picnic hamper to order. I'll come to your place, save you going out of your way. What time would suit you?'

He'd followed her out of the kitchen and now stood, looking slightly bewildered, in her living room.

'Here's your hat and there's the door,' he said.

'I beg your pardon?'

'You're getting rid of me, aren't you?'

It was her turn to look bewildered.

'Did you want to stay?'

She watched as his blue eyes absorbed her question, searching her face as if there might be a hidden meaning.

'No, not really,' he admitted, but the words held no conviction, which made her silly heart think things it shouldn't think—like the possibility of his enjoying her company! Which would be okay as long as she didn't start assuming it went deeper than enjoyment.

'Then off you go,' she said briskly, all but sweeping him towards the door. 'I'll be at your place at eleven tomorrow. That will give us ample time for a stroll through the formal gardens before we spread the tartan rug.'

He went, but not before offering his hand, taking hers and shaking it, then holding it for a moment as he thanked her once again.

The gesture caused severe internal strife and it was only by thinking hard about her dirty laundry that she was able to douse the excitement.

By eleven the next morning, thanks to constant reminders of the past disasters when her heart had ruled her head, she had herself under control again. Or thought she had until he opened the door. He was wearing dark blue denim jeans, well washed and soft so they clung to his long legs, a lighter blue chambray shirt which made his skin look more tanned than normal, and had a sweater the exact colour of his eyes slung around his shoulders.

If he'd looked spectacular in a suit, she now discovered that, in casual clothes, he was breathtaking.

'Good morning. We're all but ready, picnic basket in the car. Did you find somewhere to park?'

Nikki knew if she tried to speak while her breath was

fluttering in her lungs, she'd make a fool of herself, then made a fool of herself anyway, nodding, then shaking her head, finally summoning up enough air to make words work.

'I wasn't certain about the parking in the square so I caught the tube.'

She clutched her American jacket with its dangling strips of leather and beads tight across her chest. She'd chosen clothes she hoped might impress Jasmine, and now regretted it. How could she condemn a man as gorgeous as David Campbell to spend the day with a woman who looked as if she dressed in things Oxfam threw away?

'I like that jacket. I wish Mum would let me wear stuff like that.'

Jasmine saved the day. She appeared behind David, looking even more beautiful than Nikki's first impression of her—if that was possible.

'I've got another one just like it you could have,' Nikki said, knowing she'd never want to wear it again. 'But I doubt if it would be much use to you in the wheelchair—all the beads and strings would stick into your back.'

Meg had appeared behind her and the look she gave Nikki suggested the jacket would end up in the rubbish bin if ever it did find its way into their house. But David had caught on and the smile he gave Nikki made her glad she'd agreed to help. Okay, so her head was going to rule her heart this time, but would it hurt her heart to have just a little flutter over him in the short time he'd be around?

Yes.

'You'd better sit in front, Nicole, as you're our guide,' David said, then he turned to Jasmine. 'Out, kid, I need to pack this contraption.'

For a moment it seemed she might object to his suggestion, and the look Meg gave him showed whose side she was on. With her mother fussing over her, Jasmine stood up, her filmy, ankle-length skirt disguising whatever obvious deformity there might be in her legs.

Ignoring the little drama being carried on, doubtless for his benefit, David folded the chair and carried it down to the car. Following his lead, Nikki also ignored the pair making their slow way down the six steps to pavement level. She waited until they were on flat ground, then followed, taking the front passenger seat as ordered.

The atmosphere in the car was as unpicnic-like as any Nikki had ever encountered, although London had turned on a spectacular summer's day, with blue sky, fluffy white clouds, and probably bird song if it could be heard above the city noises.

'As it's Sunday and there won't be much traffic, I'd suggest you head towards the hospital and I'll direct you from there,' she said to David when he'd shut his relatives into the back seat and taken his place beside her. She turned to include the other two passengers. 'We'll go along Bayswater Road past Hyde Park and Kensington Palace Gardens. Have you visited them?'

'Mum likes shopping but most shops are boring,' Jasmine informed her, putting an end to that opening bid.

Some project! Nikki thought, but she wasn't ready to give up yet.

'The other side of the park you get Knightsbridge and Kensington Road. Although Knightsbridge is a bit upmarket, further along Kensington Road you get some really great stores, funky clothes, way-out accessories. A lot of young designers share space there so you can see a wide range of fashion.'

The bright info-chat didn't garner a reply but Nikki sensed a slight interest.

'Of course, a lot of places have steps so it would be hard to see the best of them in the wheelchair. I guess it limits all the things you do. Unless you can use a stick or crutches at times—that would help, but you'd need super-strong arm muscles for that. Do you belong to a gym? I go to a great one not far from your place—heated indoor pool and all. I can get a guest membership for you while you're here, if you're interested. You, too, if you'd like,' she added, twisting awkwardly in the seat to include Meg in the invitation.

'I can't go to a gym with my legs,' Jasmine told her, unwittingly giving Nikki the opportunity to pounce.

'Oh, no?' she said, hoping she sounded polite as well as disbelieving. 'I thought David said your problem was some form of JRA.' Keep it casual, she reminded herself. No one likes to think loved ones might discuss them with strangers. 'Most of the teenagers I know who have it or have had it use the gym to get out of doing boring exercises at home. I mean, there's fantastic music to work to, and so many other people of all shapes and sizes around. It gives them a buzz, especially when they can do better at some of the equipment than people who have full use of all their muscles.'

She waited a heartbeat, then added a goad to national pride, 'Of course, things might be different in Australia.'

'We have excellent gyms in Australia,' Meg said stiffly.

Jasmine added, 'And I'm joining one when I get home, aren't I, Mum?'

Satisfied with her opening salvo, Nikki stopped talking for long enough to check where they were. She gave directions to David and saw his left eyelid flutter downward in a wink, although he didn't for a minute take his eyes off the road or betray the slightest interest in her conversation.

Content to let things rest for a while, she took on a tour-guide role, pointing out the suburbs they were passing through, explaining they were heading towards Chiswick, then would cross the river at Kew Bridge.

'The river winds its way through the city so you can come across it in unexpected places. There are some good boat trips you can take,' she said as they crossed the bridge, 'or you can hire a launch and explore the upper reaches. That's a fun weekend.'

She waited for Jasmine to say she couldn't go on a boat in a wheelchair, and when she didn't Nikki wondered if the girl's determination to stay on wheels might not be as fixed as David suspected.

They parked the car, and Nikki climbed out, wondering how they'd manage wheelchairs and hampers. Then she had a great idea. David had envisaged her making friends with Jasmine and helping her that way, but perhaps making an enemy of her, goading her into doing things, might be equally effective.

'What a good thing you're on wheels,' she said cheerfully as Meg helped Jasmine out of the car. 'We can rest the hamper across the arms of the chair. That'll save your uncle carrying it.'

'But it's far too big. I won't be able to see around it,' Jasmine protested.

'Oh, I'm sure you'll see enough,' Nikki said, cutting ruthlessly across the objections both David and his sister were about to make. 'Or perhaps you could walk a little way and we could wheel the hamper. Just until we find a shady spot where we can picnic, then I'll stay and guard it, and you can have the wheelchair back while you take a look at the gardens. There are a lot of Australian plants and trees in the glasshouses, although I don't know if you'll be able to go into all of them with the chair.'

She'd only just finished the sentence when Meg seized her arm and dragged her to one side.

'I can't believe anyone working in the medical field could be so insensitive,' she hissed at Nikki. 'We try not to make a big thing of her disability. Of course she can't have that huge hamper resting on the chair in front of her.'

Nikki darted a quick glance at David, who looked as if he agreed with his sister—at least about the hamper.

'Why?' Nikki asked, hoping she looked as innocent as she was trying to sound. 'It would rest on the handles, not hurt her at all.'

She waited for Meg's reply, but guessed there wouldn't be one. It was obvious Jasmine fancied herself as the beautiful crippled maiden, taking refuge in her chair so she could be both pitied and admired. Unfortunately, Meg seemed to be going along with the image and, as Nikki had planned, a large picnic hamper would ruin the effect.

'I can carry the basket,' David offered, but Nikki shot him a fulminating glance and bulldozed aside this weak compromise.

'No, no, try it on the wheelchair. Are you going to sit in it or walk a short way, Jasmine, because if you're going to sit you'll have to get in first, before we balance the basket?'

Nikki knew she was being pushy to the point of rudeness, but had no intention of weakening now she'd begun this battle. The more Jasmine walked, the better she would be, and if David Campbell wanted her help to get his niece mobile, then he'd have to go along with her.

Jasmine looked to her mother first, but Meg had tentatively lifted one corner of the basket and now seemed doubtful about her brother's ability to carry it.

'You *can* carry it, can't you, Uncle David?' Jasmine pleaded.

By now they were all gathered at the rear of the Range Rover, Jasmine clinging to her mother's arm. Nikki gave David a swift kick in the ankle, and as he turned towards her to protest she scowled threateningly.

Tell her no, she willed him, and saw from his face that he was wavering—and annoyed with Nikki for putting him in this position.

She kicked him again.

'Well, it would be easier if we could rest it on the chair—it's a fair weight,' he said. 'And I seem to have this bruising on my ankle which would make it even more difficult.'

He matched Nikki's scowl with one of his own, but at least he was going along with her.

'Well, I'm not sitting in my chair with that great thing in front of me, so I guess I'll have to walk.'

She clutched pathetically at her mother's arm, and Nikki collected another two scowls.

She pretended not to notice, helping David balance the hamper on the chair, but as Jasmine and Meg walked ahead of them towards the gates she saw the stiffness in Jasmine's movements and guessed she'd be in real pain. Particularly as she'd been allowed to get away with this nonsense of not walking for too long.

As they dithered at the gates, paying entry fees and getting the wheelchair through, she decided it might be time to divert the girl's mind from her self-pity, and moved closer to her.

'Gosh, it's getting warm,' she said, silently chuckling to herself as she remembered how hopeless she'd been in drama classes at school. She stripped off the suede jacket, revealing the full glory of the band displayed across her chest.

'You've got an All Saints T-shirt,' Jasmine said, pain swallowed up by surprise and envy.

Nikki held the bottom of it out and squinted down at it as if she needed to check what she was wearing.

'Oh, this old thing,' she said. 'All Saints, is it? Do you like them?'

'Like them, they're the best,' Jasmine said in tones of breathless awe.

Nikki hid a grin. For the first time since they'd met, Jasmine sounded like a normal teenager.

'I might be able to get you one—a T-shirt—if you'd

like,' Nikki said in her most offhand voice, turning to help David with the wheelchair and hamper, deliberately moving away from Jasmine so if she wanted to pursue the matter, it would be up to her to make the next move.

'Aren't you going too far too fast?' David demanded, hustling her ahead of the others so he wouldn't be over-heard. 'Overdoing things? I mean, the child hasn't been out of this chair for months, and you're expecting her to walk miles in her first day.'

Nikki squared up to him.

'Do you want me to help or not?' she demanded, deter-mined not to be put off by the plea for mercy she saw in his blue eyes. 'For a start, she's not a child but an adoles-cent, entering what is probably the most manipulative stage of her entire life, and secondly, she's been walking up and down the steps where you live. You said so yourself! Thirdly,' she ticked it off on her fingers. 'Well, I can't think of a thirdly right now.'

Mainly because of the way he'd been looking at her, or the way she thought he'd been looking at her. Kind of smiling, as if he found her anger amusing, but acceptably so. Enough warmth in those blue eyes to send her breathing off rhythm again.

Then he glanced beyond her to where his sister and niece were progressing with agonising slowness along the path, and any hint of amusement disappeared from his eyes.

'There's a tree over there. We'll put the picnic basket down and she can get back into her wretched chair,' Nikki muttered, waving her hand towards the ample shade thrown by a leafy oak. 'I'll stay guard and you can all have a look around.'

He seemed put out but in the end agreed, wheeling the chair towards the tree.

'I don't want to see this dumb park,' Jasmine announced

as she and Meg joined them in the shade. 'I'll stay here. Could you please spread the blanket for me, Uncle David?'

I have to give her a point for manners, Nikki decided, standing back to see how this little scene might play out.

'You can't stay here on your own,' Meg fussed.

'I'm happy to stay with her,' Nikki said. 'I've been here dozens of times, but you won't want to miss the roses. David has a map, he can take you there, and through the glasshouses, unless you'd like to leave them 'til later when Jasmine could go with you. After lunch the hamper won't be as heavy and David's ankle might be feeling better so he could carry it.'

She spoke guilelessly but knew from David's glance he'd caught on to the next stage of her plan—abandoning Jasmine to the enemy.

'Come on, Meg, let's go look at roses, though I doubt anyone has roses as lovely as yours.'

He took his sister's arm and led her away, and Nikki chuckled.

'What's so funny?' Jasmine demanded.

'Oh, your uncle soft-talking your mother. I think perhaps all humans are manipulative when it suits them.'

'Manipulative?'

It was an opening Nikki felt compelled to take, no matter how slight it might be.

'We work things out so they suit ourselves—a lot of the time. Take your wheelchair. You obviously can walk, but you've decided you look less disabled sitting in a chair than hobbling along either with or without a stick. It looks more romantic to sit in a wheelchair and have people feeling sorry for you. That's manipulating people's emotions.'

'It hurts me to walk. You wouldn't know, you've got good legs, not twisted knees and ankles like mine.'

'I know I have good legs, and, no, I can't even imagine how it must be to have to put up with both the pain and the embarrassment, but I know if it did happen to me I'd hate to think I just sat around all day, waiting for my legs to become so stiff and weak I'd never be able to walk at all.'

'That won't happen for ages. I might decide to walk again before that.'

'If what I saw of your walking today is any indication, then I'd say a year, tops, before you can't walk at all. Then, whenever you want to go anywhere, even down to the shop, you'll be dependent on someone lifting you in and out of your chair.'

Jasmine sat up on the blanket and looked around as if she'd like to find something she could throw.

'How would you know?' she asked. 'My uncle's an expert and he's not always telling me to get out of my chair.'

'Isn't he?' Nikki said mildly, deciding she'd done enough goading for the moment. 'Oh, look. Did you see the squirrel? There must be a couple of them in the tree and he's decided to come down and inspect us.'

'But he's so tiny!' Jasmine said. 'I thought they'd be like possums—much bigger than that.'

Her voice made the little creature turn his head to one side, looking at her with a quizzical glance, then he scampered back up the tree, disappearing from sight.

'There are deer further over in the park, and we might see pheasants as well,' Nikki told her.

She moved so her T-shirt was more clearly visible to Jasmine, and chattered on about the delights of the park, went on to mention some of the equipment in her gym, casually dropped a second invitation for Jasmine to visit it some time, just for a look, then asked, 'What other music do you like? What groups and singers?'

It was the perfect opening, and for the next forty minutes all she had to do was make agreeing noises as her companion extolled the virtues of various weird-sounding musicians.

'Goo Goo Dolls?'

'Yeah, they're good,' Jasmine said, and sang a few lines from their latest single.

'Hey, you can sing,' Nikki said, clapping her appreciation.

Jasmine blushed.

'I'd like to do more with music and singing. You know, work in a recording studio or something, but Mum says that's not a real career and anyway there aren't that many jobs.'

'Oh, I don't know,' Nikki argued. 'Music is a huge business these days—there's the video side of it as well. I would think there'd be thousands of jobs in related fields. It's just a matter of finding out about them.'

She waited a split second then said in an elaborately offhand voice, 'I could probably arrange for you to visit a recording studio and possibly get you into the audience at one of those TV shows that play videos and music.'

She saw Jasmine's eyes, so like her uncle's, light up with delight, and added the kicker.

'But it would have to be a deal. Look, Jasmine, you're fourteen and you're obviously not stupid, so there's no point in my trying to go about this in an underhand way. Your uncle asked me, because I'm a physio and work with kids who have arthritis, if I could work out some plan to get you out of the wheelchair.'

She could tell by the mutinous expression on Jasmine's face that she was furious, but held up her hand to stop her objecting.

'You must know he's right when he says you'll be far worse off if you stop moving naturally, if you stop walking and refuse to do your exercises. He only wants what's best for you in the long term.'

'He doesn't understand how dread it is to hobble,' Jasmine wailed. 'No one does!'

'Of course they don't,' Nikki agreed, 'but he does know that you're too young to decide you want to be dependent on people for the rest of your life. He knows how much you're limiting your potential.'

'Well, it's none of your business anyway,' Jasmine snapped. 'And you can just tell him it's none of his either. You can forget your gym and making me walk all over the place because I'm not going to.'

'Okay,' Nikki told her. 'If that's how you feel, that's fine by me. I'll tell him I tried, that's all I could do.'

She plucked a few clover heads from the grass and began to thread them into a crown.

'How do I know you could get me into those places anyway?' Jasmine asked, after so long a pause Nikki had begun to wonder if she'd gone too far too fast.

'Into a recording studio? Maybe to an All Saints session?' She shrugged elaborately. 'My brother's an agent for a lot of bands. Actually, he gave me this T-shirt but I don't know if he manages them or if someone gave it to him. He's probably got more.'

Bait the hook again and let it dangle.

'Your braids are dreadfully untidy. Why don't you take them out?'

Once again Nikki smiled to herself. The insult in the words showed Jasmine was still thinking through the suggestion—trying to find another way she might get what she wanted, but not wanting Nikki to think she was hooked.

'I'm keeping them in because two little girls in one of my arthritis groups plaited them for me. They've both been affected in the small joints of their fingers so it was a big effort.'

'My hands are okay,' Jasmine said, offering two small,

neat hands with slim, tapering fingers for Nikki's inspection.

'They're beautiful,' Nikki told her. 'Look at them next to my whoppers.'

She spread her hands beside Jasmine's, measuring them up for size.

'It must help you when you massage people,' Jasmine said, and Nikki felt a surge of triumph that she was finally breaking down the barriers between them.

'Helps me threaten them if they don't do their exercises,' she joked and Jasmine laughed, then pulled up some clover of her own and began to thread her own crown.

'What kind of deal?'

It had taken her so long to ask, Nikki thought she might have forgotten where the conversation had begun.

'Oh, one where you exercise more. Every day—full stretches and the whole bit—no compromise. As I said, I'd be happy to take you to the gym with me. Exercising there is fun, not like exercising at all. I could go through a typical programme and we'd decide together what equipment and classes would be best for you.'

'And what would I get out of it?'

Jasmine's voice told Nikki that she wasn't exactly delighted by the prospect—in fact, she sounded surly enough to still turn it down.

'What would you really like? A visit to a recording studio? TV studio? Live concert? Leonardo di Caprio in person?'

'You know Leonardo?' The wonder in the wide blue eyes made Nikki regret her flippancy.

'No, I made that one up, I'm sorry! That was unfair. But I'm sure I could organise the other things for you. Are there any concerts coming up? Anything on with bands you like?'

'I don't know the things that might be happening in

London, and we're only here for the summer,' Jasmine admitted. 'How can I find out?'

Nikki hesitated, wishing she'd listened more closely to Andrew when he talked about his job.

'There must be magazines about the music scene, pop culture, that kind of thing. I've never really been into it, but I'll find out and let you know what's on when we have our first gym visit.'

'I haven't said yes,' Jasmine reminded her. 'And how can you take me to the gym when you go to work all day?'

'We'd have to go before I go to work. Early.'

'I don't get out of bed until nine o'clock. Why can't we go after your work?'

Nikki considered the question for a moment. Was this a simple objection or was Jasmine trying to regain some control over the situation? She decided it was a simple objection and as such could be overridden. If the girl suffered pain during the night, early mornings would be impossible for her. Perhaps it wasn't a control issue.

'We'll work something out,' she told her new and reluctant friend. 'I'll need to do one session with you, then perhaps I can arrange a personal trainer to look after you.'

She had no idea what such a luxury would cost, but if David wanted results he'd have to be prepared to pay for it.

'The evenings are bad for me. I often have to work late, and now your uncle's got this panel idea where young people who've suffered arthritis as children, or still have the disease, are going to debate various issues, so I'll probably be working even longer hours.'

Nikki intended the grouch purely as an added excuse to not go to the gym in the evenings, but Jasmine's frown suggested she'd picked up on it.

'I'm a young person with arthritis,' she muttered.

'That's right,' Nikki agreed, wondering where this was leading.

'He didn't ask me to be on this stupid panel.'

Uh-oh!

'Perhaps he thought you wouldn't be interested,' Nikki offered, then she realised that here was the perfect opportunity to add another straw to the wheelchair's back. She'd really goaded Jasmine enough for one day, but if the girl was interested...

'I guess he thought you wouldn't be a good example— using the wheelchair when he keeps telling his patients they mustn't use one, except on special occasions or as a last resort.' Knew she'd gone too far when she saw the tears sparkling on the thick dark lashes. She put her arms around Jasmine and held her close.

'Oh, Jazzy,' she murmured, using David's diminution of the pretty name. 'I realise how rotten it must be for you, being different from the others in your group, having to put up with pain and bent legs and all the rest of it. But giving in to it isn't the answer. We could all give in when things get difficult, then we'd never get anywhere. Do you think All Saints were an instant success? I bet they were knocked back by a dozen radio stations, band venues and recording studios before they got their start.'

She felt the thin shoulders moving as the girl sobbed, so she held her tight and let her cry.

'I miss my dad,' a quavery voice said eventually. 'That's when I decided not to walk again. I thought if he didn't love me enough to stay, then why should I bother?'

Nikki helped her straighten up and offered a tissue for the mopping-up operations.

'That's really tough,' she told Jasmine. 'And nothing anyone can say or do can make it easier.' She smoothed the lustrous hair with soft fingers. 'Physios don't have exercises for that kind of pain.'

Jasmine smiled through the bleary remnants of her tears.

'Hey, don't cry again,' Nikki teased her gently. 'If you do, I'll have to hold you and this T-shirt, which I was going to give to a beautiful young Australian I've recently met, is already very wet.'

'Would you really give it to me?' The accompanying smile was a better effort this time. 'Don't you want it any more? A used one is so much better than one that looks brand-new.'

She sounded like a child again, the child she still, in part, was, and Nikki hugged her.

'I'll not only give you this one, but I'll see if I can get a new one you can keep as special, with the girls' signatures on it.'

Rash promise, but she was so excited at getting this far with Jasmine, she'd have promised her the moon.

Only Jasmine didn't want the moon, she wanted her father.

The thought curbed Nikki's excitement.

CHAPTER SEVEN

'I FULLY expected to see the blanket awash with blood,' David muttered in her ear as he knelt beside Nikki to unpack the hamper.

'There are a few drops here and there,' Nikki told him, under cover of Meg's delighted recital about the beauty of the roses.

'And?' he persisted, flipping the tablecloth across to Jasmine and waving his hands to indicate she should spread it.

'There's a tentative truce that's in existence because of bribes I hope I can pay.'

Nikki took the cutlery and plates from him and moved so she could set them on the tablecloth. As a teenager she'd hated the thought that 'grown-ups' might be discussing her, and didn't want Jasmine to get the impression she was under discussion.

The lunch was spectacular, although Nikki suspected that David's company would have made fish-paste sandwiches taste like caviare. She relaxed and enjoyed the meal, feeling the warmth of the sun's rays where they filtered through the leaves, hearing David's voice as a counterpoint to the rustling of the squirrels and the call of the birds, barely listening to the family's conversation as she cherished her own secret delight in his presence. Her heart was weaving unlikely fantasies her mind knew were dangerous.

Too dangerous!

'I've over-eaten now,' she complained to no one in particular. 'I'll have to walk it off. What about you, Jasmine? Want me to steer that elegant machine of yours as far as the glasshouses? We can park it outside and do a short walk in the heat while you show me which plants grow in Australia.'

'I would have thought the glasshouses would be wheelchair accessible,' Meg sniped. 'From what we've seen, Australia is way ahead in that kind of thing.'

'I don't mind a short walk, Mum,' Jasmine told her, earning Nikki a black look from Meg, and an expression of almost comical surprise from David.

'See, I'm going to keep my end of the bargain,' Jasmine said as they moved away from the shady tree.

'I hope so,' Nikki said, but she knew it would be hard going, particularly as Meg seemed intent on keeping her daughter dependent.

So she, bruised from her divorce, felt needed?

Nikki sighed. She didn't want to get involved in that scenario!

Or any other scenarios which would put her into close contact with David Campbell. In fact, the sooner she arranged Jasmine's gym therapy and set her up with a competent trainer, the sooner she could back out. Concert tickets could be posted, arrangements for studio visits made over the phone.

Which would restrict the danger times to working hours, when she should be busy enough to ignore the worst of her symptoms.

'Natalie Imbruglia's Australian.'

Jasmine's statement brought her back to the present, and the answer to her 'who's Natalie Imbruglia?' question got them as far as the glasshouses, where Jasmine, true to her word, parked her chair and walked with Nikki, pointing out eucalypts, bottle brush, macadamia, and an assortment of smaller Australian shrubs and ferns.

'I don't know all their names, but Mum would. She's dead keen on gardening.'

'Perhaps she'd like to do a garden tour—take a coach around some of the famous English gardens.'

'It means I'd have to go with her, now Uncle David's working,' Jasmine complained. 'And I'm not going to sit on a coach with a lot of old ducks and go gaga over gardens.'

Nikki chuckled.

'I don't blame you,' she said, then turned as she heard Meg's voice.

'Oh, Jasmine, your skirt, it's trailing in the mud.'

'It'll wash, Mum,' Jasmine said, but Meg wasn't going to be appeased, catching up the trailing skirt and tutting over it.

'Come on, we should go home. If I rinse it straight away it might come out. David's taken the hamper back to the car, we can see the rest of the park some other time.'

Nikki said nothing, backing off both physically and metaphorically as she sensed her guess about Meg might be closer to the truth than she'd realised.

'I'll drop you and Jasmine home—it's been a long day for Jazzy,' David said over his shoulder to Meg as they drove back. 'Then I'll take Nicole home. She came down on the tube.'

'I'd like to ride on the tube while I'm here,' Jasmine piped up. 'It's so famous, I'd die if my friends asked about it and I had to say I hadn't been on it.'

'Maybe towards the end of your stay,' Nikki suggested, turning to smile at Jasmine, and, as Meg wasn't looking, to wink.

Jasmine winked back.

'Nikki says I can go to her gym,' she announced. 'And maybe get a personal trainer.'

Nikki shrivelled into her seat, aware of the reception this announcement was likely to receive. She'd intended working up to it with David, and letting him explain to his sister.

'I'm sure Nicole is too busy to take you to the gym,' Meg said repressively. 'And a personal trainer in London would cost more than we can afford.'

'Daddy gives you money to spend on me!' Jasmine retorted, her voice regressing to a childish plaint.

Nikki waited for David to buy into the argument, but he was staring resolutely ahead as if the Sunday-quiet road required super-human concentration.

She wanted to say it was only a suggestion, but knew if she backed down now Jasmine would retreat from the deal, and be stuck in her wheelchair until someone with more sway than Nikki could persuade her out. By which time, it could be too late.

'Left at the next roundabout,' she said to David, to get him back into familiar territory.

He nodded and turned, but didn't otherwise acknowledge that she'd spoken.

Until they'd dropped Meg and Jasmine at the house—Jasmine giving Nikki a hug before she clambered out of the car—and were driving towards Hampstead.

'Do you think perhaps you overdid things, setting Jasmine and Meg at odds? Wouldn't it have been easier to check with Meg what was acceptable before making arrangements with Jasmine?'

His voice was mild, but it didn't deceive Nikki for one moment.

'Do you want my help or don't you?' she demanded, the frustration of being so close to him for so long sliding into anger. 'You knew what you were getting when you asked me to help you. You don't approve of my methods of treatment but because Mark—a man—told you they worked, you've reluctantly enlisted me. And now you're stuck with me, because that young girl has a lot of spunk and I'm going to get her out of that wheelchair for good. Now, will her family pay for a personal trainer for her or am I going to have to see if I can wangle some funds out of the hospital?'

'You can't do that, she's not a patient,' David objected.

'Don't bet on it,' Nikki warned him. 'I could make her a patient really quickly. Get her in for some intensive rehab—in fact, that might not be a bad idea. It would give her mother some time to herself, maybe get away on a garden tour, and—'

'Hold on a minute!'

He pulled into the drive leading up to her flat, and parked where she'd indicated the day before. Then he cut the motor and held up one hand.

'You're going too far, too fast. Get Jasmine into hospital? Send Meg on a garden tour?'

'Jasmine said her mother loves gardens and gardening, and getting away on her own might be just what she needs. She'll meet new people with similar interests and enthusiasms. I know there are a few organisations that run garden tours. Shall I find out?'

He was leaning against the steering wheel, but facing her, with a strange expression on his face.

'Are you always this ruthless at arranging other people's lives?' he asked. 'Was it only yesterday I asked you about helping Jazzy? Surely not! I don't believe even you could have turned this family on its head so swiftly. Meg said, after you'd hijacked Jasmine and taken her to the glasshouses, that the child had been crying. If I hadn't restrained her, she'd have gone after your blood right then and there.'

'I didn't make Jasmine cry,' Nikki protested, but she knew she had. 'Well, not in the way you're thinking. Not by sticking pins in her.'

'Not physically,' David countered. 'But having heard a few of your verbal jibes...'

He was frowning, as if he'd found her behaviour distasteful, and that upset her far more than the words. She flung open the door of the car.

'If you want my help, then you'll have to let me do it my way, but if you prefer to keep shuffling around Jasmine's delicate little ego and your sister's growing dependency on her role as ''Jasmine's mother'', then go right ahead. I've got better things to do with my time than waste it on people who don't want to be helped.'

She climbed out and was about to slam the door shut behind her when he reached over and stopped the movement.

'I didn't say I didn't want your help, and I'm sorry if I seemed to be questioning your methods. What can I do to make it up to you?'

There was something personal in the words. Nikki knew that because they made her skin tingle, but she couldn't take it that way—couldn't let him get any closer in case holding back the physical demons became too difficult.

'You can pay for the personal trainer I'm going to find for her, and organise someone dependable to be at home with Jasmine while your sister gets herself a life—I'll help out there with the names of some good agencies—and ask Jasmine to be on your panel.'

'Ask Jasmine to be on my panel?'

'Exactly! Here you are, scouring my files for likely contenders and you've got one sitting in your own house. It's ideal. You'll have Tom as the voice of young men and Jazzy as the voice of younger women.'

He was stunned enough to loosen his grip on the door, so she pushed it shut—gently—and turned towards her flat, not waiting for a response, knowing she didn't want to watch him drive away.

It was like fighting a battle on several fronts, Nikki realised—a week and a lot of grief later. First, she had her own internal strife caused by her attraction to David, then she had Meg's resistance to everything she suggested for Jasmine, and thirdly—

Well, it wasn't that David was being deliberately obstructive, but he did seem to question everything she did, whether at work or with his niece, and he was around a whole lot more than Mark had ever been.

Or was it simply that Mark fitted better into her working life, a friend and colleague, as comfortable to have around as old bedroom slippers? Whereas David Campbell was like the sleek evening sandals she'd once bought for looks rather than common sense, and which had caused her pain from the first time she'd worn them.

She grinned to herself as she made her way towards his office, wondering what he'd think about being compared to silver and diamanté footwear.

'Ah, Nicole, I was just coming to find you.'

His door had opened as she raised her hand to knock so she was left with a raised fist poised above his chest, and a startled whisper of surprise hovering on her lips.

'I wanted to thank you for your input into the panel. Last night's discussion went really well, and from Jasmine's conversation on the way home I'd say your friend Cecilia could replace the band in her affections.'

'Cecy knows more about Andrew's life than I do, so she's up on all the latest in the music world. She was able to tell Jasmine what live concerts are scheduled and also promised to get her tickets for whatever she could.' She hesitated, aware this could undermine her own plans. 'I'd better talk to her about those promises. For one thing, I don't want Jasmine to think she can circumvent her deal with me, and for another, I can't see Meg being all that happy about taking her daughter to rock concerts.'

'Well, don't look at me!' David grumbled. 'I get headaches living in the same house with Jasmine's CDs. Her player only works on full volume, so I can imagine how loud the bands she fancies must play.'

'Maybe Harry could take her.' Nikki spoke the thought aloud, but didn't realise it until David spoke.

'Who's Harry and how did he get into this conversation?'

'Oh, that's what I wanted to see you about. He's the personal trainer I found for Jasmine. He works with other clients at the gym and comes very highly recommended. I introduced him to Jasmine and she seemed to like him but, as either you or Meg will be paying him, I was going to bring him over to your place tonight to introduce him. If that would suit you, of course.'

David said nothing, but Nikki, with her body finely tuned to every nuance in his, could feel an uneasiness in him. See doubt in his beautiful eyes.

'You're doing an awful lot for a family that mean nothing to you,' he said. 'I know I asked for your help with Jasmine, but it seems to me you're putting yourself to a whole heap of trouble for her.'

'I like her,' Nikki said, pleased it was the truth. Although she was coming to realise that if David Campbell asked her to dance naked on the helipad on the hospital roof, she'd probably agree.

But that was her own folly and none of his business.

'And Meg? Do you also like her?'

'I haven't done much for Meg,' Nikki protested, pushing the toe of her shoe against the door jamb as she considered her failure to break through Meg's icy disapproval. 'Apart from getting the brochures for the garden tours. And as she won't consider leaving Jasmine with a stranger, it's not likely she'll go on any of them anyway.'

In fact, her relationship with Meg was non-existent, although the woman was always polite when Nikki called to collect Jasmine, or drop her home. At first, Nikki had put it down to what Meg saw as her interference in Jasmine's life, but the occasional remark about David made her wonder if Meg regarded her as some kind of threat where her brother was concerned.

If she but knew…

'Deep thoughts?'

She glanced up to find David studying her again.

'Not really.' She brushed aside his interest and moved away from the ambient influence of his body. 'I've told Harry eight-thirty. Jasmine seemed to think you'd be finished dinner by then.'

'We'll expect you at eight-thirty, then,' he said, with his usual courtesy, but the tension she'd felt earlier seemed to linger between them.

'Are you not happy about this personal trainer thing? Is that what's worrying you?'

She was watching him as she spoke so saw him blink as if her question had startled him out of some very different thoughts.

'No, the personal trainer thing is fine,' he said, then, to her surprise, he leaned forward and once again kissed her on the cheek.

Well, she assumed he'd been aiming for the cheek, but she moved at the same instant and his lips brushed across her mouth, firing such a dizzying sensation she had to clutch at the door jamb to steady herself.

Not that he seemed affected in any way. He simply straightened, raised those aggravating eyebrows in a silent question, then murmured, 'I'm sorry. I shouldn't have done that right here and now. I know you're not happy about there seeming to be anything between us.'

Nikki gazed at him in stunned disbelief.

'So where or when should you have done it?' she demanded, then realised it wasn't a very sensible conversation to be having with someone who affected her as badly as David continued to do.

'Oh, somewhere, some time,' he said vaguely, then he took her arm, pulled her right inside the office, shut the door, and repeated the kiss. Only this time his lips lingered long enough to fill Nikki with a feverish need, which she possibly betrayed, for she certainly kissed him back.

Then, belatedly, she remembered reserve and reticence and her determination that he shouldn't learn how she felt about him, and she drew away, opening the door and stepping backwards through it.

He watched her movements with a kind of detached interest, then he said, 'Thank you,' in his polite way, as if she'd taken part in some experiment for him, before turning back into the office and shutting the door between them.

'Thank you? Thank you for what?' Nikki muttered to herself as she marched back towards her office.

'Talking to yourself now? That's a really bad sign.'

She scowled at Crystal and slumped into the chair, then she folded her arms on the desk and dropped her head to rest on them, breathing deeply but quietly because she didn't want her sister-in-law making any more smart comments.

'Are you sick?' Crystal sounded concerned but Nikki couldn't answer—not truthfully. If she said yes, Crystal would want symptoms and Nikki's symptoms all added up to the one diagnosis she didn't want to reveal—not to her family, who'd suffered through her other bouts of it, and particularly not to the object of her…what? Obsession?

She hoped not, but it was close, considering how her heart behaved whenever he was around. Even when he wasn't present in the flesh, but striding through her mind like an unwelcome wedding guest.

No, don't even think of the word wedding. It must have been the kiss that had allowed her thoughts to make that leap.

She'd keep out of his way. That was what she'd do.

Introduce Harry tonight then make sure all contact was strictly business. It shouldn't be too difficult.

'I'm not having Jasmine running around with that testosterone-laden hunk of muscle,' Meg declared when Jasmine had taken Harry upstairs to see the posters Cecilia had dropped at the house earlier in the day. They were in the study where the introductions had taken place, the ambience of the room failing to warm Meg's welcome.

She had addressed her brother with this announcement but, seeing his uncertainty, Nikki stepped into the breach.

'Why not?' she asked. 'Just because he looks like a young Greek god doesn't mean he's going to rape or pillage your daughter.'

'I think pillaging was much the same as robbery,' David put in, and earned a scowl from Nikki and a snort of disbelief from Meg.

'You know what I mean,' she said to him. 'Now, say something, David. Tell Nicole he's not suitable.'

Nikki turned to him and showed she could raise her eyebrows—though possibly not as elegantly as he performed the feat.

'You've read his references,' she challenged. 'Do you think he's unsuitable?'

He looked from her to Meg, then back to her again.

'I imagine Meg is concerned Jasmine might be foolish enough to fancy herself in love with him.'

'Well, that would be foolish,' Nikki said, letting sarcasm drip from every word. 'Terrible for her first crush to be on someone who's actually clean, not on drugs, into fitness, *and* a thoroughly nice young man, when most young women of her age would take one of the less savoury pop idols as their icon.'

David's frown told her she'd scored, but she knew he

was uncomfortable at being asked to mediate between her and his sister. She took pity on him.

'Look,' she said, addressing Meg this time. 'I realise you must feel very protective of Jasmine, particularly as her disability renders her more vulnerable both physically and emotionally, but Harry's totally reliable and completely trustworthy. I've checked him out with a dozen people and I know he'll be kind to her even if she does develop a crush on him. And a little crush could be an advantage as far as her exercises are concerned, because she'll work even harder for him if she's keen to impress him.'

'I don't like any of it,' Meg said, then she turned to David. 'You barely know this woman, yet you're letting her run our lives. We were doing fine until she came along.'

He stepped towards Nikki as if to protect her from his sister's ire, but, as he'd said much the same thing to her, Nikki didn't expect him to spring to her defence.

Not that he actually sprang. More like drifted.

'I asked Nikki to help me with Jasmine's attitude to exercise. You should be grateful she's willing to give so much of her time and energy.'

'Well, I'm not!' Meg told him, and she walked away, not quite slamming the study door behind her. Nikki frowned at the door.

'What happened in her marriage? Do you know? Was there a third party involved?'

'Now there's a conversational switch,' David said, smiling at her in such a way she remembered the kiss and her toes went tingly. 'As far as I know, there wasn't anyone else on either side. It was just a general breakdown. I know Paul was devastated, but Meg? She's obviously not happy, but whether that's because of the divorce, or Jasmine's illness—I don't know.'

He sighed and retreated behind the desk again, dropping

down into the deep leather chair and waving for her to sit opposite him.

'I don't understand other people's relationships. In fact, I'm not too good with my own.' He looked at her from across the desk, studying her intently, then continued, 'I married my first girlfriend when we were both eighteen. We went to school together and it seemed the natural thing to do, although both our families were up in arms over our age. It was good. We were happy. Perhaps not as happy all the time as I tend to think we were, but marriage certainly worked for me. She died of breast cancer when she was pregnant with our first child. I was twenty-five, and a doctor, and couldn't do a damn thing to save her.'

Nikki felt pity for him well up in her chest but knew he wouldn't find it acceptable, so she went for practical instead.

'How old are you now?'

'Ten years older, and, yes, you do get over grief. It becomes less intrusive in your life, although Anne's memory will be with me for ever. But it's not like a ghost hanging over my head or haunting the present. More like a silent companion in my life.'

The words were so poignant Nikki had to swallow hard before she could speak, turning the conversation abruptly back to where it had been because to think about his Anne would be more than she could handle right now.

'I think it's possible Meg's using Jasmine as a crutch— that's why she's upset about other people having influence over her.'

There, it was out!

David frowned, then seemed to consider the suggestion.

'It's quite likely, but what can we do about it? Are you going to pull another rabbit out of your hat? Perhaps another brother who will have Meg forgetting all her disappointment and swooning at his feet? Is love a cure for everything that ails the world?'

He was teasing her, but she resisted the temptation to tell him it would go a long way towards curing a lot of it.

'I haven't got another brother—apart from Gerald who's too busy with school and football and cricket to see the attraction in an older woman.'

'I was joking,' David said with an alarmed look on his face.

Nikki grinned at him.

'So was I,' she assured him. 'Although, maybe you've got a point. Maybe a man's the answer.'

'Don't even think about it,' David growled. 'For all I know she's still in love with Paul.'

'But that's even better,' Nikki told him, forgetting her determination not to become too involved in this family. 'Jasmine misses him terribly. I don't suppose we could get him over here for a short visit? He could mind Jasmine while Meg does a garden tour—no, that won't work, we'd need the two of them together—'

'*We'd* not be doing anything,' David responded. 'And, anyway, Meg's already agreed do a garden tour. Her friend Lucille arrives next week. She's quite happy to babysit Jazzy while Meg goes away.'

Lucille! The woman he was going to marry! Here! In London!

The exclamations clamoured in Nikki's head. She swallowed the panicky flutters in her throat, told herself it would make resisting him so much easier. She stood up, wanting to run screaming from the room, but deciding a dignified retreat might be the better option.

'How nice!' she managed. 'Now, I must be on my way. Harry should be finished inspecting Jasmine's treasures by now. We're going to stop for a drink on the way home.'

Not that Harry drank anything but freshly squeezed juice,

but David didn't know that, and Nikki wasn't going to tell him. She needed a drink—possibly more than one.

Then she remembered where this conversation had begun. With Meg. And, although she wasn't all that fond of David's sister, she was concerned about the woman's obvious unhappiness. Her own unhappiness she couldn't cure, but maybe Meg's...

'Does Paul—the ex—like gardens? What you could do is get him over here, and book him on the tour, and—'

'No!'

It wasn't so much the word as the way he said it that made Nikki pause.

'You don't think so?'

'I don't think I should interfere in their lives,' he said firmly, 'and, before you get any more ideas into that lovely head of yours about involving Jasmine in a similar deception, let me tell you—'

Lovely head?

Nikki's thoughts were caught by the phrase, her mental processes diverted into thinking whether he might have meant it. If he did find her reasonably attractive—when she wasn't dressed as a clown.

She missed whatever threat he was issuing, but the idea of involving Jasmine wasn't half bad. The man might not fly over to England because his ex-wife was unhappy, but if he thought his daughter needed him?

Not half bad!

bur David asked about and Nikki wasn't going to tell him. She freed herself gently—pushing him down on the bed—and they began an angaged physical conversation, as her soul still with Max. And suddenly she wasn't all that fond of David's smile, the way it did that to the women and those little niggles, her own inadequacies, that silky virgin

CHAPTER EIGHT

ONCE Harry was established in Jasmine's life, and monitoring her exercise programme, Nikki was able to withdraw, so she saw less of the family—or the member of it she wished to avoid—outside the hospital.

Avoiding him at work was more difficult, but not impossible for a lateral thinker, once she set her mind to it. By sending advance notice of the change to her patients' families, she was able to move some of her therapy sessions to the pool. Hard to imagine a man who came to work each morning in an immaculately cut suit joining her in the chlorine-tainted humidity of the pool.

Then she organised a series of home visits to new patients, something she and Crystal did from time to time.

'For what purpose?' David asked, when she dutifully explained they would be away from the hospital for a few days.

'We both check out the physical environment. I look at the layout of the dwelling, to see what natural activities might be included in the exercise programme for the child. You know, trees for a swing, a big or small yard. Flat or house, detached or semi.'

He looked confused and she tried again, but being near him always affected her rationality as well as her hormones and she had a struggle with the explanations.

'If a patient's family lives in a council flat which is up three flights of steps then, providing the child isn't carried, he or she is getting enough leg exercise walking in and out of the home.'

'Are there such places? Wouldn't you have a lift for three flights?'

Nikki sighed. She'd tried to talk Crystal into telling David of their expedition, so she'd be spared this proximity, but her sister-in-law was proving surprisingly obdurate these days, and was already peeved that Nikki had changed the home-visit schedule.

'Yes, there are such places, although most are ten storeys and do have lifts. But that was just an example. I mean, it's stupid saying to a parent, encourage him to ride his bike, if the only place a child could possibly ride a bike is on a balcony three feet by five feet that's usually cluttered with washing lines.'

From the look on David's face, her explanation wasn't helping.

'Wouldn't the parents tell you?'

'That's what I assumed until I started home visits. No, they don't. Sometimes because it doesn't occur to them that I might not know, or perhaps because they don't want to admit they haven't perfect facilities for their child's reha-bilitation. But I think the main problem is that the parents only absorb about ten per cent of what we say to them in a hospital atmosphere.'

He smiled, and caught her stupid heart unawares, so it did a cavorting routine that left her breathless.

'I read a study about that once,' he agreed. 'It listed the range of emotions relatives experience in a hospital envi-ronment. I think anxiety was number one, but it included both intimidation and false bravado, and with all that con-tradictory emotion raging through them I was surprised to find they remembered anything at all.'

Her body, starved of contact by her avoidance tactics, urged her to continue this discussion, but her head re-minded her of why she was getting out of the place. If anything, the tension she felt when she was near him was increasing—a sure sign inoculation by proximity wasn't working.

'Crystal checks to see what aids might be installed, or what special utensils might be needed. Railings in the bathroom are the most common, sometimes a sling arrangement over the bed to help a child in and out. Everything is designed to keep the patient as independent as possible.'

'Do you do school visits as well? Check out the children's physical environment there?'

She grinned at him.

'Your interest's showing! It wasn't just to help Mark out that you stepped into his shoes, was it? I can tell by the way your eyes gleam when you question people in the unit about roles and responsibilities. You're filing it all away in that computer you call a brain. Are you doing more writing? A book on children with arthritis? Or setting up a similar unit back in Australia?'

The slight movement of his shoulders was an admission in itself.

'We have similar units in the larger hospitals, but with a population as widespread as Australia's it's hard for families not living in the cities to access regular therapy sessions.'

'Which means the parents miss out on the support that attending sessions provides, the opportunity to talk to others who have similar problems with their children. I can understand that, but where does my home visiting fit into this?'

She was ready for the smile this time, but steeling herself against it didn't diminish its effect completely.

'Some other organisations, like the cerebral palsy associations in different states, have a team of therapists making regular visits to country areas. I'd like to set up a similar team for children with arthritis. They could meet with the health department therapists in the regional centres to pass on the latest information or techniques, and also do some hands-on work with the children and their families.'

'A kind of therapy flying squad?' Nikki teased, then regretted the impulse as his blue eyes gleamed in response and sent her pulse-rate sky-rocketing again. She'd caught him looking at her like this from time to time—in an assessing kind of way, as he had the day he'd kissed her. But there'd been no mention of that since, and no repeat kiss, so she told herself it was imagination and that it was just as well his Lucille was arriving any day.

Keep a distance, she reminded herself.

'Yes, we do visit schools as well,' she said, belatedly answering his question in an attempt to get the conversation back to where it had been before *she* had turned it more personal. 'It's an important part of the child's physical environment, and the easier we can make it, the better for successful integration.'

He nodded, his eyes once again scanning her face, but his expression giving nothing away.

'Well, enjoy your freedom,' he said. 'The panel's meeting on Thursday evening this week. I assume Carol advised you of the change. You'll be able to attend?'

Could she miss it? She thought of Tom, Jasmine and Cecilia, not to mention Phil Edwards, the physician—four people who were on the panel thanks to her persuasion. No, she couldn't back out at this stage.

'I'll be there,' she said.

'Perhaps—' he began, then his pager bleeped and he excused himself and turned away, leaving Nikki wondering what he'd been about to ask.

Something she wouldn't have liked hearing, if the grave expression on his face was any indication!

Nor could she ask what he'd been about to say when they did meet up again on Thursday evening.

She'd dropped Crystal home after the last home visit, then driven back to the hospital in the late afternoon to write up her notes and recommendations, check on the mail, and see patients on the ward. By six, lunch seemed a long time ago, and dinner even further removed.

Deciding she needed a snack if she was going to offer the panel anything beyond stomach growls, she detoured via the washrooms where she had a quick wash, brushed her hair into a shiny fall and moistened her lips with a pale pinky gloss, then walked out to the mini-mall in the front entrance in search of sustenance. A health bar, or an apple? She was debating choices when an excited voice calling her name made her spin around.

Jasmine was approaching, on foot, not in the wheelchair, one hand resting lightly on the arm of an attractive young woman.

'Hi, Nikki. Come and meet my friend Lucille. She's coming to the panel tonight, just sitting in because she's a dentist, not a doctor, but as Mum's away I couldn't leave her alone, could I?'

Nikki smiled at the breathless introduction, and held out her hand to Lucille, wondering how it was possible to feel the blood leaking from the cracks in her heart.

'I'm perfectly willing to sit outside this panel,' Lucille told her. 'In fact, knowing David, it's quite likely I'll be made to do just that. We've always kept our professional lives separate.'

Her smile lit up her tawny brown eyes, and teased Nikki into smiling back.

'It's Harry's birthday tomorrow so Lucille's going to help me choose something nice for him at Foams.'

Jasmine broke in again, waving her hand towards the little shop that sold soft toys and personal gifts like body lotion and aftershave.

'Something for Harry or another animal for your collection?' Nikki asked, remembering the little squirrel Jasmine had discovered in the shop on her way through the mall before the first panel meeting.

'Perhaps you should help us choose,' Lucille suggested, her soft voice so friendly and inviting Nikki wanted to hit her.

'No, I'm in search of food,' she said. 'I'll see you later. I'm quite sure David won't make you sit outside.'

'Of course he won't,' Jasmine agreed. 'Mum thinks Lucille and Uncle David will get married soon.'

If Jazzy hadn't put it into words—

Confirmed what David himself had said—

If only Lucille weren't so nice—

Bother!

Nikki's hunger had gone but she sought refuge in Dunwoody anyway, only it wasn't Dunwoody she walked into, but the little post office, something she worked out when she saw the stationery and cards on the shelves where she'd expected health bars to be.

'May I help you, Miss Barclay?'

Nikki glanced up from her detached perusal of a sorry-about-your-accident card that had an elephant sitting on a hapless human of indeterminate sex, and shook her head, amazed as ever when Mr Goode remembered her name.

'I don't think so,' she said, her gaze moving on to sticky tape and string, thinking how much easier life would be if she could just patch up the cracks in her heart with sticky tape or glue. 'I think it's because she seems so nice, that I'm devastated,' she said, unaware she'd spoken aloud until she noticed the concern in Mr Goode's kindly eyes.

'There, there,' he said. 'You've probably been working too hard. Perhaps an early night.'

Nikki recovered sufficiently to smile at him.

'Now, that *would* be a good idea!' she said. 'Unfortunately, it's not possible, but I can always fall back on the good British traits of reserve and reticence, can't I?'

'Of course, Miss Barclay,' he agreed, but she knew his eyes, behind their gold-rimmed frames, were puzzled.

She walked back towards her office, considered raiding the emergency make-up supplies Crystal kept in the filing cabinet for a lipstick brighter than her gloss, and perhaps some mascara to make her lashes look longer. A light dusting of powder?

Then she laughed at herself for even thinking that way. She had no illusions about her looks, nor false modesty. She was good-looking enough—even typically 'English' with her straight fair hair, clear skin, pale eyes more grey than green most days.

But not breathtakingly beautiful the way the Campbell family was, nor devastatingly attractive like Lucille.

And neither a brighter lipstick nor longer eyelashes would change that fact.

Plunged into gloom by her ruthless self-appraisal, she dawdled along to the treatment room where they held the panel debates.

David's raised eyebrows suggested she was late, but the welcome noises from the other members drowned out any rebuke he might have made.

Lucille was present—not condemned to sitting outside the door at all—and Nikki strained to hear an indication of his feelings for her in his voice as he introduced her.

As a friend!

Well, he'd hardly introduce her as his future wife at a work-related meeting like this, Nikki told herself.

'We've met,' she said, when David reached her name, then her mood lightened slightly as she watched Phil all but falling over himself to get the chair next to the newcomer.

'She's just as nice as she looks,' Cecilia whispered to

Nikki. 'I was talking to her earlier. She said she'd be happy to take Jasmine to the recording studio—even to the rock concerts if Andrew can get some passes.'

'She's a bloody marvel!' Nikki whispered back, then glanced up to find David watching them.

'Ready?'

The arched eyebrows lifted, but beneath them the blue eyes were cool.

'Whenever you are,' Nikki said, using cheek to allay the devastation in her heart.

They launched into a general discussion on steroids, beginning with the differences between the medical ones and those used for body-building.

'I'd be on them all the time,' Tom joked, 'if I thought they'd give me muscles. I'd be all for their use from a very early age.'

Jasmine giggled, and Nikki thought how good it was to see her behaving like a normal adolescent. At least someone was benefiting from David Campbell's visit to London!

'When I had a lot of inflammation, I often had steroid injections into my joints.' Cecilia took up the conversation. 'The others have probably had the same thing. Why is that treatment used fairly freely when other steroid treatment is considered such a big deal?'

She turned to Phil who managed to drag his attention away from Lucille for long enough to answer.

'Oral or injected steroids—prednisone is the one used—are systemic. They are absorbed into the blood and travel throughout the body, into all the tissues and organs. The injection you have into a joint to relieve pain and inflammation is localised. Very little chemical passes into the body. It's the same with the steroidal eye drops used to treat iritis in a lot of arthritis patients—they're local and aren't absorbed into the blood so they don't cause the serious side effects.'

Tom picked up the list of side effects they'd been given on the first evening, and asked whether all of these would occur in every patient.

'And I'd like to know if studies have been done on how long you have to be on steroids to suffer from all these dire consequences,' Cecy added.

It focussed the attention on Phil, as the physician included to talk about steroids and their effect on the body. Which gave Nikki time to study Lucille, and as an adjunct, or so she told herself, David's body language towards her.

Not that she could read anything from either of their attitudes. Lucille seemed more interested in what was being said around the table than in the man—lover?—from whom she'd been separated for some weeks.

While David—well, Nikki had admitted long ago that he did reserve and reticence far better than she did.

Except for that one time—the strange kiss. Not the first one in the doorway—she was willing to admit it had been an accident. It was the second one, when he'd pulled her inside the office and made a proper job of it. That kiss had her puzzled.

And kept her awake at nights.

'Do you agree, Nikki?'

Nikki caught the question in time to answer, 'Yes, of course,' then realised she'd made a fool of herself when Tom gave a shout of laughter.

'I'm sorry. I—I must have missed the bit before that,' she stuttered, made even more embarrassed by the assessing way David was regarding her. Surely she hadn't been gazing blankly at his lips while her mind had relived that moment?

'That's okay, you've had a busy few days and are probably tired.'

'And hungry, from the way her stomach's growling,' Jasmine suggested, earning herself a black look from Nikki.

'Could we get off my physical state and back onto the subject we're supposed to be debating?' she said crossly.

'We were talking about going out to eat somewhere,' Tom told her. 'All of us. Jasmine suggested McDonald's and everyone but you groaned and said no way.'

'Well, I like McDonald's,' Jasmine protested.

'I think I'll go home,' Nikki said, knowing she'd never survive two or three more hours of conviviality with Lucille and David included in the party. 'I've got to wash my hair.'

It was probably the feeblest excuse she'd ever used, but no one argued or protested that her hair looked beautiful just the way it was. Not that she'd expected such a reaction.

She packed up her notes and stood up, then hesitated. She'd have liked to ask Tom, who was now discharged from hospital, how he intended getting home to the far side of London, but, knowing his fierce independence, she decided against it. The young ones were arguing over where they'd go, Phil and David discussing cars and who would go with whom.

Was she foolish to refuse? Probably. Nikki headed away from the table before she could change her mind.

Mrs Wilkinson, a parent included on the panel, also opted out, saying her husband would probably kill the kids if she wasn't home to supervise their baths.

Nikki stood aside to let the other woman go ahead of her through the door, then felt a hand on her shoulder and needed only the tremor of delight that shivered through her blood to know it was David's.

'Will you be in tomorrow?' he asked. 'I'd like to talk to you. Perhaps lunch in the coffee shop? One o'clock.'

Her brain couldn't dredge up another feeble excuse and she heard herself agreeing.

'Fine,' he said, the chocolate of his voice dripping across her skin. Then he patted her, removed his hand and turned

away, leaving her to find her way through the door and out
of the building.

It's only work, she told herself—repeatedly. Yet she
couldn't stop feeling excited about the meeting, about having a chance to sit and talk to him—just the two of them.

It's an indulgence you can't afford, her head said, but
she knew the price she'd pay, and looked forward to it
anyway.

'I remembered you saying how pleasant it was out on
the river,' he said, when they'd made greeting noises at
each other the following day, and had ordered lunch. 'I
wondered if you'd like to do a boat trip on Sunday?'

His blue eyes were enhanced by the blue colours in his
tie, and his skin still retained its healthy tan although he'd
now been in England for weeks. These and other impres-
sions jostled in her mind as she considered the invitation.
Reminding herself that the inoculation idea wasn't working,
she decided on avoidance instead.

'We'd have to check out how accessible the boat was
for Jasmine,' Nikki suggested, more to delay a decision
than for therapy reasons. 'I know she's progressing well,
but steep stairways could be risky.'

She saw a smile twitching at the corners of his mouth,
and twinkling in his eyes.

'I wasn't thinking of taking Jasmine,' he said.

Nikki was about to ask why when she realised it wasn't
any of her business. She'd been distracted by the twitch
and twinkle—only momentarily, of course.

'Just Lucille and Meg? And me? A day surrounded by
women?'

He looked disconcerted, which was good as she felt that
way most of the time she was within a radius of one hundred feet of him.

'I wasn't planning on asking Lu or Meg either,' he said.

'I thought we could go.' He waved his hand across the table as if to show her who 'we' were. 'Just you and I.'

Disconcerted didn't begin to describe her feelings at that point.

'Why?' she asked, perhaps a tad bluntly.

'The chicken lasagne for you?'

David again used a hand movement, this time to indicate to the waitress it was his meal. He waited until Nikki's bowl of pasta arrived and the waitress had departed, then said, 'Why not? Is there some reason why I shouldn't invite you out for a day on the river?'

She frowned at him, annoyed to have the question thrown back at her.

'I asked first,' she told him. 'Why would you?'

He shrugged his impossibly broad shoulders, then grinned at her.

'Back when it occurred to me, it seemed like a good idea. Now we're getting into the metaphysics of it, I wonder.'

Well, at least he hadn't told some tepid lie about enjoying her company.

And what about the woman he was supposed to be marrying?

'I would have thought, with Lucille here, you'd be wanting to spend whatever free time you have with her,' Nikki said tartly, pleased to have found a diversion she could use.

'Meg returns from her garden tour tomorrow. I thought she and Lucille would enjoy some time together.'

'Noble of you!' Nikki muttered. The answer to her 'why' question was now abundantly clear. Having decided—with rare male tact, she had to give him that—that the two women might like to spend the day together, he'd simply looked around for a companion.

Then something synapsed in her fogged brain.

'I can't go Sunday. It's family dinner day.' Then she

remembered something else and frowned at him. 'I thought Crystal had invited you. I'm sure I remember giving you a warning look when I heard her prattling on about open house at the Barclays' and you ignoring it and saying you'd like to go. In fact, she included Meg and Jasmine, and presumably Lucille too, if she knows she's staying with you...'

The words trailed off as the enormity of what Crystal had done finally occurred to Nikki. Back when it had happened she'd protested, but since then she had been too busy to think much about the repercussions of the invitation. Now, instead of avoiding him, she'd be expected to make polite and welcoming-type conversation with him during their monthly family get-together.

And with the disdainful Meg, and the gorgeous Lucille!

Bother didn't seem strong enough!

'That's this Sunday?' he asked, looking quite as shocked as she was feeling.

'If it's the third Sunday in the month, then yes.'

'Oh, well, perhaps we could do a boat trip some other time.'

Did he sound relieved or was she imagining it? She replayed the words in her head, testing each of them for undertones, so missed the beginning of his next sentence, catching only '—Saturday evening.'

She looked blankly at him and shook her head, which, for some reason, now had him frowning.

'Why not?' he demanded.

'Why not what?' she asked, all innocence.

It broke him up completely. From frown to laugh in a split second—joyous, unrestrained laughter that made her shake her head again, this time in bemusement, while everyone in the café turned, eyebrows rising politely as they failed to catch the joke.

If there was a joke.

'You are an impossible woman,' he said, when he'd recovered sufficiently to speak. 'Where do you go when you disappear behind those filmy grey eyes of yours? What's going on in your head that's so distracting you could be on a railway track and unaware of your surroundings?'

Filmy grey eyes?

'Railway track?'

His laughter had subsided but his amusement lingered in his eyes, his voice.

'Well, at least you heard that,' he said. 'But admit it, you didn't hear a word earlier. Didn't hear the question I asked.'

Laughter was all very well, but it made the person being laughed at uncomfortable. It also made the laugher infinitely more attractive. She had to sort this out, and fast.

'About going on a boat trip?' she guessed, then realised she'd gone too far back. 'About Sunday lunch?'

He'd stopped smiling now. In fact, he looked quite serious. Especially when he leaned forward and rested his hand lightly on top of hers.

'I asked if you'd like to have dinner with me on Saturday evening instead,' he said. 'Apparently the idea held no appeal whatsoever, if the vigour of your head shake was any indication.'

Nikki withdrew her hand from beneath his and tucked it into her lap. She shouldn't have had it on the table in the first place.

Say no, her brain told her. Or at least ask him about Lucille's position in his life before you say yes.

'Our lunch is getting cold,' she said instead. 'Perhaps we should concentrate on that.'

'For the moment, Nikki,' he agreed, and she didn't need to run the words over again in her head to hear the implacability in his voice.

It's a thank you gesture for helping him out with Jasmine, Nikki told herself. The boat trip was a good choice as it would have been in daylight—casual. Then, when you reminded him of lunch, he was thrown and dinner was the first thing that occurred to him.

This explanation was acceptable enough to make eating a possibility, and, once she'd tried her pasta, it was delicious enough to finish.

'Shall I pour your tea?' David asked, and Nikki smiled as he'd said the same thing the first time they'd lunched together. On that dreadful day when she'd recognised her symptoms.

'Thank you,' she said, manners helping out in this awkward situation. 'And thank you also for the dinner invitation, but you don't have to take me out. I was happy to help you—help Jasmine.'

Now *he* shook his head.

'What on earth has my dinner invitation to do with your helping Jasmine?'

She didn't know why he was getting exasperated. She was the one battling to retain her cool here.

'I thought it was your way of saying thank you. Asking me out. A gesture, you know.'

He smiled and reached out again to take the hand she'd again left carelessly within his reach.

'It is not a thank you, nor a gesture, but an invitation. Don't men still ask women out to dinner in London? Is it not the done thing? Has feminism swept away all male-female rites and traditions?'

'An invitation?' she repeated. 'To dinner?'

Heavens, if he'd thought her vague earlier, what must he be thinking now?

And why wasn't she saying no?

She considered the word—only two letters, one syllable, easy enough to say—but couldn't bring herself to come out with it.

Not yet.

'What about Lucille?'

The growl—for there was no other word to describe his reaction—startled her.

'Honestly, Nicole, carrying on a conversation with you is like wading through custard, and don't you dare ask me if I've ever waded through custard. Or worse, fix me with those lovely eyes and say why! I ask a simple question and we get so far off track I start to wonder about my sanity. What *about* Lucille? What does she have to do with this?'

Once again heads turned in their direction. At least they were entertaining the lunch crowd.

'I would have thought she'd have a lot to do with it,' Nikki said stiffly. 'After all, you did tell me you thought you'd probably marry her.'

'Did I say that?'

He both looked and sounded shocked.

'You did,' Nikki assured him. 'And then Jasmine said much the same thing, as if it's been a foregone conclusion between you for some time.'

He now looked even more shocked, raising his free hand and running his fingers through his hair.

'I suppose— At one time— I might—'

Nikki retrieved her hand—again—and patted his.

'I'm sure you'll sort it out,' she said, just as Claire Oates appeared in the doorway of the coffee shop, scanned the customers, then made a beeline for their table.

'Have you got your bleeper turned off?' she asked David. 'I've been trying to get on to you. Mark's been on the phone. He's ringing back in five minutes.' She glanced at her watch. 'Actually, about two minutes.'

David rose to his feet, glanced at Nikki as if uncertain who she was, then followed Claire out of the café.

'Leaving me to pay for his lunch!' Nikki told the waitress. 'That's nice, isn't it?'

'Well, he's so handsome I'm sure if you didn't want to pay for it, there'd be plenty of others as would.'

'True,' Nikki admitted, and as she handed over the necessary change she reminded herself there'd be just as many jumping at a dinner invitation from the man.

So why hadn't she?

Why had she dithered and thrown up objections?

Because you don't trust yourself with him, that's why.

It was the truth, but suddenly it didn't seem like a strong enough reason. Perhaps he'd forget, wouldn't mention it again.

Perhaps…

CHAPTER NINE

DAVID may have been avoiding her as assiduously as she was avoiding him, Nikki decided as she slipped away from work at the early, for her, time of five-thirty. Her heart suggested his invitation—no, more his uncertainty over the invitation—might show he was interested in her, but her head warned her to stay clear.

At least until he'd decided whether or not he intended to marry Lucille, and preferably until he realised that besotted wasn't all that bad.

Which could be never.

That was the strangest part of this particular attack of love. It had made her notions of a marriage built on good friendship and mutual interest quite laughable in her mind. Now, for some reason, she wanted love, a besottedness to meet and match hers—the kind of love that crossed all barriers, moved mountains, made strong men tremble, and weak women strong.

If that was possible!

The thoughts occupied her on the drive back to her flat, where common sense dictated she throw some clothes into an overnight bag and get out of the place. David Campbell wasn't going anywhere for another couple of weeks. If he was developing an interest in her, there was still time to see where it would go.

As far as mountain-moving? her head asked and she chuckled to herself. She doubted it, but maybe there'd be room for compromise.

She drove towards the M1 which would take her to her parents' home in St Albans, then decided she was in no

139

mental state to tackle the motorway and took the old roads home, battling slowly through the congested traffic as Londoners fled the city for the weekend.

It was a cowardly thing to do, and because she wasn't usually so craven it bothered her, so she argued it back and forth in her head until she reached the outskirts of the beautiful old city. The rush of joy she always felt when she returned home filled her, washing away her negative thoughts, the arguments and doubts.

'Oh, darling, what a lovely surprise. I'm so glad you decided to come earlier. Crystal appears to have asked half the hospital to lunch on Sunday so you can give me a hand.' Her mother hugged her hard then kissed her cheek. 'Actually, I'm quite pleased as I've seen this darling dress in a shop in town and having some extra visitors gives me an excuse to buy it. We'll both go in first thing in the morning and you can tell me what you think.'

Nikki felt the warmth and security wrap around her, and the smiling serenity on her mother's face reaffirmed her belief in love. Her parents had been besotted with each other for close to forty years. She greeted her father, then took her bag upstairs to her old bedroom, still furnished with the remnants of her childhood life. She glanced at herself in the mirror, at the smock she'd put on for her afternoon therapy session and worn home because it needed washing.

So far, David Campbell had seen her in a clown's costume, and jeans. She washed her face and hands, then went down to join her parents for a pre-dinner drink.

'Where did you see this "must have" dress, Mum?' she asked. 'Would the shop have anything that might suit me?'

She felt as if she were seventeen again, ten years stripped away in the uncertainty of love. And her mother didn't by so much as a blink of an eyelash reveal her surprise or pleasure in Nikki's taking an interest in clothes. Well done, Mum!

'There's a great skirt and jacket. I thought of you when I saw it. It needed someone much taller than me to carry it off.'

'And since when did my tomboy betray an interest in clothes?' her father asked, walking into the room to catch the conversation. 'Would you like a drink?'

Nikki smiled at the frowning glance he received from her mother, and said yes to a drink.

'I'd love a glass of wine if you're opening some for dinner,' she told him, ignoring the clothes question. Her mother, whose instincts were well-enough honed to guess there was a man involved, would no doubt fill him in later.

Gerald came in as they were finishing their drinks, and Nikki relaxed and let the security of being 'home' fold around her. They had a happy, talk-filled dinner, then she excused herself and went to bed. This had been the best idea she'd had for a fortnight.

Setting out on the shopping expedition dampened down her enthusiasm for home, reminding Nikki of similar forays into fashion in her youth, her mother bubbling with enthusiasm while Nikki alternately argued and sulked.

First she was introduced to Diane, the woman who ran the small boutique her mother had chosen as a starting point.

'She's a perfect Summer,' Diane announced, after peering at the skin on Nikki's face and inner arm, then examining her eyes intently.

Nikki turned to her mother, who nodded complacently.

'Diane does your colours then shows you what you can wear. She's even divided her shop into the different seasons so, once you know your colours, you just look in that part, and choose clothes from there.'

Nikki glanced around. She'd noticed as she'd walked in

that the sections of the shop were labelled by season and had wondered why anyone would stock winter clothes in summer. Now she looked more closely, she could see summer clothes in the winter section. Colours by the season! What would her mother come up with next?

'Here's the suit. I'd guessed you were summer and checked through what was here last time I visited. Look, it's got trousers as well as a skirt, a jacket and one of those new long-line cardigans that only people your height can wear really well. And I thought this blouse and this T-shirt for mixing and matching.'

Nikki watched in horror as her mother pulled garment after garment from the racks and handed them to Diane to hold. Perhaps it was time to take control.

'That suit's a kind of beige colour, Mum,' she pointed out. 'You've told me I look like a washed-out dishrag in that colour.'

Her mother was unperturbed.

'No, dear, this is rosy beige, isn't it, Diane? It's the best neutral for you, apart from white, of course. And the good thing about it is that it's made from some kind of knitted material so you can throw it on the floor in the corner of your room when you take it off and pull it on again next time you go out and there'll be no wrinkles.'

The heat of mortification washed into Nikki's cheeks. She'd regressed again, from seventeen to seven, when 'pick up your clothes' had been her mother's most frequent refrain.

'And it's a dream for travelling,' her mother added. 'Diane says you can roll it into a little ball and shove it in your suitcase and it comes out totally creaseless. Oh, dear, is creaseless a word, do you think?'

Nikki knew the artless question was intended as a diversion, but she wasn't falling for it.

'I'm not buying all those clothes,' she warned her maternal relative, but, rather than make a scene in the shop, she followed Diane and the clothes into the changing room.

'I've added a couple of fine-knit, lightweight jumpers that will also look good with the suit,' Diane told her. 'I guess it's not a colour you wear often, but the brown would look great on you and totally change the look of the suit to give the impression of a bigger wardrobe.'

'I don't go to enough places to need a big wardrobe,' Nikki told her. 'And I rarely travel so the scrunching-it-up pitch is really wasted on me.'

Diane smiled at her.

'Then just try them all on to please your mother,' she suggested. 'I'll get the dress.'

'What dress?' This was serious panic time.

'It's a lovely dress—in muted lavender and orchid tones—very summery and elegant but pretty at the same time. Your mother said immediately that it was made for you, and she's right.'

She walked out, pulling the curtain behind her, leaving Nikki and a pile of clothes she didn't want or need.

Except perhaps something for Sunday lunch.

She stripped off and tried the suit first, matching the trousers with the fine-knit rose-coloured top her mother had chosen, and adding the long-line cardigan.

The colour in the top lent a warm blush to her usually pale skin, and the line of the cardigan and trousers was sleek and elegant, yet casual enough for lunch in the garden. She tried the brown roll-neck sweater next and knew immediately she could wear it on a boat trip up the river— with Jasmine and Meg and Lucille as well as David. If he mentioned it again.

Or she could suggest it to Jasmine...

A pale aqua patterned top made her eyes look greener, and certainly gave a new look to the suit, although that top was better with the skirt and jacket—

I'm falling for my mother's propaganda, Nikki thought, but as the clothes both looked and felt good on her she wasn't sure she could muster up the will to fight against the make-over.

Diane's arm slid into the cubicle and deposited the lavender dress on the hook.

'Can I take anything for you?' she asked, not intruding but hovering in case Nikki needed help.

'All of this,' Nikki told her, pushing the discarded garments into her arms. 'And although it's a great selection and I really like the look of it, I don't think I need that many clothes. This is more my mother's idea than mine.'

Diane smiled as if she understood about mothers and disappeared, leaving Nikki to try on the lavender dress.

'Oh!'

The tiny sound escaped her lips as she surveyed a self so altered she wasn't certain she recognised her. The garment must have been woven with magic for it clung seductively to her shape, diminished what she always saw as excessive height, and overall made her look so feminine—so beautiful—she had to close her eyes and then open them again to make sure it wasn't a dream.

'Come out and show us,' her mother called, and, not even considering a refusal, Nikki slipped on the backless sandals thoughtfully provided by Diane for people who'd come shopping in their brogues, and glided out into the shop.

The tears that started in her mother's eyes were enough to confirm her own impression of how she looked.

'Oh, darling,' her mother whispered. 'You're beautiful!'

I'm beautiful.

It was a new concept for Nikki, one she found difficult to grasp immediately.

'Believe it,' Diane said. 'You look absolutely stunning in that dress. It was made for you.'

Stunning as well?

'I'll take it,' she heard herself say as the words started a revolution in her head. If she was beautiful and stunning, and a nice person, besides, shouldn't she be fighting for the man she loved? Especially now he seemed confused about his plan to marry Lucille. It was time for war, and these were battle clothes. 'I'll take the lot. We'll come back and get it all later, but right now I need to find a hairdresser who can fit me in some time today.'

Her mother looked as surprised as she felt, but Diane came to the rescue.

'My sister works from home and she had a wedding booked for today which has been put off because the bride had to have emergency surgery for a burst appendix. She'll come to your home. Do you just want a cut?'

Nikki was about to nod when her mother, recovering with a vengeance, answered for her.

'And highlights. Silvery streaks to lighten the ash colour. Can you arrange that for us, Diane? We'll be home by one. And we'd better take the clothes so she knows what shoes she needs to get.'

Which left Nikki with nothing to do but hand over her credit card and turn away as the massive total was printed out.

Bits of the old Nikki were secretly appalled at her rash behaviour and uttering dire warnings about falls, but she was carried along on a wave of confidence, created mainly, she had to admit, by the sight of a few tears in her mother's eyes.

Strappy leather sandals made her legs look impossibly long and would go with both the trousers and the skirt, then, thinking it was a long time since she'd spent money on good shoes, she found more sedate court shoes to wear with the outfits to work occasions when jeans and a smock weren't the right attire.

Evening footwear was harder, but her mother found the sleek black shoes on a sale table, reduced from an astronomical amount to something that made Nikki wince only slightly.

'We'll take the lot,' her mother said, getting into the grandiose jargon of the expedition. 'Then we'll buy some smoked salmon and go home and give the boys a treat for lunch.'

Nikki chuckled, suddenly light-headed with anticipation. Okay, so she might be riding for a fall, but this time she wasn't going to fall without a fight.

Sunday dawned bright and clear—well, it had actually dawned a trifle misty but cleared itself up by nine, and by eleven was a beautiful summer's day.

'I guess we're ready,' Nikki said to her mother, surveying the array of cold meats and salads they'd made for lunch in the garden. The table in the arbour was already set up buffet-style with crockery, cutlery and napkins. All they had to do later was transfer the food to it so everyone could help themselves.

'Your father and Gerald have set up the picnic tables in the shade. I guess everyone will find somewhere to sit.' Her mother fussed some more over the punch bowl which was awaiting the last-minute addition of ice chips and champagne.

'You're getting into a tizz, Mum,' Nikki chided, sliding an arm around her mother's shoulders and giving her a hug. 'You've had more people than this to sit-down Sunday dinners, so why the panic today?'

Her mother turned and looked at her, then smiled.

'Perhaps because I had a feeling it might be battle stations, darling,' she said. 'Is it?'

Nikki shrugged, not surprised her perceptive parent had

honed in on her war-like metaphors. Particularly not when Crystal had, no doubt, dropped the odd hint.

'I don't know, Mum,' she admitted. 'Heavens, the entire family knows what I've been through with this love caper, and I'd hate to put you all through it again, but there's something different about it this time. He might be special, Mum.'

Her voice quavered on the last admission and she found herself folded in her mother's arms, regressing again to when a kiss would make things better.

'Well, you'd better get upstairs and put on your war-paint—or is it armour?' Her mother rejected the sentimentality first, pushing Nikki towards the stairs as she spoke. 'I'm glad you had your hair layered. I know I've always been against it because you look lovely with it done up on your head, but that feathery look is really pretty and it's still long enough for you to pull it back and look sleekly elegant. Yes, Stephanie's a genius.'

Was it a weekend for compliments, or had she been drifting through life careless of her appearance for too long? Nikki wondered when she came down the stairs a little later and earned a long wolf-whistle from Gerald.

'Wow, Sis, where have you been hiding that body?'

The question sent her into a panic and she clutched at her breast, checking there wasn't a slit in the top that revealed cleavage.

'You can't see any of my body,' she told him. 'This is neck-to-ankle stuff.'

'Yeah,' Gerald drawled, 'but it sure does it well.'

She was thrown by his comments but, as cars were already pulling into the drive, it was too late to change.

Andrew, whom she expected to notice clothes and appearance, said nothing as he greeted her with absent-minded affection.

'That new doctor chap Cecilia was talking about coming today?' he asked.

'Yes, why?'

Andrew looked startled, as if he'd not expected anyone to notice his distraction.

'Oh, nothing,' he said. 'I just wanted to have a chat to him.'

Nikki watched him walk away, heading for the bar where her normally abstemious brother poured himself a large Scotch.

Trouble with Cecy? Could Andrew be jealous of her involvement on David's panel?

She was puzzling over his attitude when Cecilia came in, explaining she'd been delayed in the garden where Gerald had wanted her opinion of the table placement.

Nikki noticed Andrew's stillness when he heard Cecy's voice. The hand that had been lifting the glass to his lips paused, then, without taking a sip, he set the drink back down on the bar, removed the top of the Scotch bottle, and poured it all back in. After recapping the bottle, he turned and crossed the room, where he lifted Cecy into his arms and said, 'Drop your sticks, Nik will stash them somewhere. I'm taking you out to a shady spot in the rose bower where I'm going to strew petals beneath your feet.'

Nikki retrieved the sticks and put them in the umbrella stand, blinking away a tear as she replayed the little scene in her mind. Whatever it was bothering Andrew, it wasn't a lack of besottedness that would part that couple.

Crystal and Peter arrived next, and, from the sound of more car doors slamming, the visitors weren't far behind. Nikki made a dash for the kitchen.

'I'll do the punch, you go and meet them,' she told her mother, who seemed taken aback to find her usually brash daughter cowering in the kitchen.

'You work with the man every day. Do you usually hide from him?'

'Just go, Mum,' Nikki pleaded, then she put her hands on her mother's shoulders and guided her towards the door.

Suddenly the war didn't seem like such a good idea, the new clothes too new, too fancy. She longed for the security and anonymity of her old jeans and smocks, but it was too late. Dutifully, she opened the champagne, added it and ice to the punch, then carried the bowl out the back door and across the lawn to the table.

Beyond the arbour, Andrew, true to his promise, had settled Cecy on a garden lounger in the shade and was strewing rose petals all around it.

He'd obviously gone mad, Nikki decided. Maybe it was some kind of genetic thing that came out in members of this family in summer but up until now had gone unnoticed because they were usually very busy at this time of the year.

'Avoiding me?'

The voice swamped her with its usual effectiveness and she turned around to face him.

'Yes—no—well, yes, I suppose so.'

He smiled at her inept stumble into speech, but his gaze raked over her with a hungry intensity that made the shiver from his chocolate voice seem negligible in comparison to what she was feeling now.

'Why, Nikki?'

She opened her mouth to say, Why what? then closed it again, determined to match her image and be cool, elegant, controlled—possibly even reserved and reticent.

'It seemed like a good idea at the time,' she told him. 'Would you like a drink? There's punch here, beer and soft drinks in the house. Did you find your way without too much trouble?'

She lifted the ladle from the punch bowl and filled a glass

for him although he hadn't said he wanted punch. He hadn't said anything. All he'd done was look at her.

'Oh, Nikki, you look wonderful. Somehow I hadn't pictured you in anything but your work clothes. That top is rad. Is it new?' Jasmine arrived with her enthusiastic praise and rescued Nikki from a situation that was becoming more tense by the moment. Although she could have chosen a better conversation opener than whether Nikki's clothes were new.

'Do you want a drink, Jazzy?' she asked, avoiding an answer. 'Not this, it's alcoholic.'

'No, thanks. There's Cecy over there, I'll go and talk to her.' She took a step towards the rose garden, then halted. 'Is that her Andrew? Your brother who knows the bands?' she asked Nikki. 'What on earth's he doing?'

Nikki felt rather than saw David move closer, and knew he was within inches of her back because her skin's receptors were doing their job with great enthusiasm.

'Strewing rose petals at her feet, I'd say,' David murmured. 'Now why didn't I think of that?'

Stepping carefully away from him, Nikki turned, but before she could question the words Meg and Lucille appeared.

Meg greeted Nikki with her usual distant politeness, but Lucille was more open in her delight with the day, the house, the garden, what she'd seen of the ancient city as they drove through—everything, in fact.

Particularly David, it appeared, when she slid a proprietary hand into his arm and said, 'Will you walk through those heavenly roses with me?'

Nikki poured Meg a glass of punch, pretending her attention was on the job while all the time she was watching the couple's casual progress across the lawn.

Lucille looked as beautiful as ever in a casual dress of soft autumn colours, and she and David looked good together although he was so tall and she was no more than medium height.

'She's a lovely woman.' Meg seemed to pick up on her thoughts. 'I don't know how I'd have got through the last twelve months without her.'

Crystal appeared and took Meg off to see the dahlias, and Nikki was left alone, wondering if she really wanted to fight a woman as nice as Lucille. Her appetite for war had dulled, and she felt like doing what Andrew had done on his arrival—pouring herself a large Scotch.

Only she'd want to drink it, not pour it back.

Thinking of Andrew, though—

She checked he was still in the rose bower. When Lucille and David reached it, Cecy could introduce him. She puzzled over why Andrew would want to talk to him as she walked back to the kitchen to bring out the nibbles they'd prepared as appetisers.

'Who's Lucille?' her mother asked, spearing straight to the heart of the problem.

'The woman he's always thought he might marry,' Nikki told her. 'Makes things interesting, doesn't it?'

'But not impossible,' her mother said. 'I've always found that people who put off marrying usually do it because, deep down, they know it's not right for them.'

'He's had the one that was right for him,' Nikki told her as a gloom as thick as the morning's mist descended on her. 'This time around he's going for companionship and mutual friends and similar interests. He's decided he's too old for love.'

'Nonsense,' her mother said. 'No one's too old for love.'

Nikki wasn't convinced, but as she strolled around the garden, offering food to the scattering of friends and family, she felt her optimism returning. Especially when she spied Lucille, Gerald and Jasmine sitting together by the old tennis court and realised David must be at large somewhere.

But he wasn't. He was with Andrew, who'd left Cecy in her bower of roses with Peter to keep her company and was now leading David towards a long garden seat near the wisteria.

He glanced up and waved to her to join them.

'I was telling David I wanted to ask him something but you're a woman so perhaps you should sit in on this.'

Nikki frowned. She'd never heard Andrew so uptight, not even before a televised live concert which, to her, was like a glimpse of hell.

'It's Cecy,' he said. 'We've reached an impasse. I want to marry her and she won't agree because she says I'm a family person and will want a family and she's not sure, after all the treatment she's had, if she can have kids.'

Nikki felt her stomach cramp with pity for her brother and the woman who adored him.

'Is that what you wanted to ask David? Her gynaecologist would be a better person to tell you that.'

'No, I've read about risks of infertility with the use of immunosuppressive drugs. Believe me, I know enough about arthritis to be able to quote the books. What worries me is the risk associated with a pregnancy.' He looked at David. 'I couldn't bear to lose her, you see,' he said simply. 'So I'd far rather not have children than cause her problems or have it lead to any hideous complications with her health.'

'She's not my patient,' David told him, 'so I have no idea of the extent of her disability. SLE can cause organ damage and if her kidneys are impaired then a pregnancy could put extra stress on them. That would be the first thing to check. I imagine she has hip deterioration because of her use of sticks, but the only physical problem that I could foresee, if infertility and kidney problems are ruled out, is having a natural delivery. And that can be overcome by a Caesarean.'

'But carrying a child? Extra weight and pressure on her joints? Wouldn't that be difficult, dangerous?'

David shook his head.

'I'm a paediatric rheumatologist, but some patients I've had have gone on to have families. I think you've got to realise that Cecy's used to dealing with the difficulties caused by her disability—in fact, I think she relishes the new challenges life is continually throwing up at her. If she's capable of having children, if she and you both want them, then, working with her rheumatologist and her gynaecologist, it should be possible.'

'She won't die?' Andrew persisted and, seeing the pain in David's face, Nikki wanted to kick him.

'No one can guarantee that, Andrew,' David replied, then he glanced at Nikki, and must have read her emotions on her face.

'Now, you go and propose to your young woman so those rose petals don't go to waste, and I'll take your sister away before she gets wound up enough to have an argument with you.'

He took hold of Nikki's arm and guided her away, leaving a stunned-looking Andrew gazing after them.

'I'm a doctor, people talk about death and dying all the time,' he told her gently, 'but I'm glad you care enough to feel upset for me.'

They walked on, David letting go of her arm to relieve her of the plate of savouries.

'Perhaps we should offer these around once again. You'll look dutiful and it might give your mother a good opinion of me.'

Nikki glanced at him but there was no expression now to be read on *his* face. Bland, that was how it looked, but still incredibly handsome.

'Ah, David, we haven't had a chance to say more than hello. Is Nicole looking after you?'

Her father crossed the lawn to greet them, and this time she *could* read the expression on David's face. His eyes were alight with mischief and she blushed as her mind picked up the connotations he might have put on 'looking after'.

'I'll take those. Mum probably needs some help.'

She grabbed the plate of savouries and made a dash for the kitchen, where she leaned her head against the refrigerator and wondered if love was worth the physical upheaval it caused.

CHAPTER TEN

THE rest of the day passed swiftly, too swiftly for Nikki as there were no further opportunities to be alone with David, although she did catch him watching her from time to time.

She was in the kitchen, rinsing plates before stacking them in the dishwasher, when he came to say goodbye.

'Meg tells me Jasmine is tired,' he said, and she straightened up to see a wry smile on his face. 'I think what she really wants is to get away before Jazzy persuades Cecilia to have her for a bridesmaid now the wedding's been announced.'

'But it's not until winter,' Nikki protested.

'Exactly. Now Jazzy's begun to enjoy herself in London, I gather she'd like to make more regular visits and this would be a great excuse for the first of these.'

He stepped towards her and turned off the water she had running into the sink.

'With air travel improving all the time, Australia isn't as far away as it used to seem.'

It was a strange comment, but one she'd have to think about later as he'd come close enough to steal the air from her lungs and muddle her brain processes with the freshness of his aftershave, and the powerful effect his body always had on hers.

Hormonal overload, in fact.

'Are you driving back to your flat later this afternoon?' he asked.

Did he want her to?

Was he going to suggest they meet?

Excitement flashed along her nerves, then conscience caught her back.

'There's a lot of cleaning up to do, then Mum will want a post-mortem of the day, and to chatter about the wedding. She'd begun to think Andrew would never take the plunge.'

She studied David's face as she explained but the only expression she could detect was what looked like approval and that couldn't be right. But before she could puzzle over it he distracted her again, this time with a light, teasing kiss, brushed across her lips, so gently a butterfly's wings would have seemed heavy in comparison.

'And you? Is she anxious for you to take the same plunge?' he asked, staying very close so she could see the darker striations of blue in his eyes.

'Andrew and Cecy have been together for ages,' she managed to mumble, made even more breathless by this personal question than she was by his closeness.

He nodded, then straightened up and said, 'Yes, time's a problem, isn't it?' Then he took her hand. 'But you're not doing any home visits this week so I'll see you at work. I've even bought myself a pair of swimming trunks and a most respectable towelling robe to go over them so I can track you down when you hide yourself away in the pool.'

He bent and kissed her again, more forcefully this time, taking possession of her lips in a masterful manner that insisted she respond. Which she did. Masterfully.

'Uncle David, Mum and Lucille are waiting in the car.'

Jasmine's voice put an end to it although David held Nikki steady as he drew away from her, and she felt a tremor in his hand that made her wonder if the second kiss had affected him as badly as it had affected her.

'I suppose we can be thankful for small mercies,' he said quietly, then he turned to where Jasmine stood in the doorway, watching them with a gleam of interest in her eyes.

'One word of what you just saw and I'll cut you off my

panel,' he warned his niece. 'This is something private between myself and Nikki—something we're still exploring, you might say.'

Jasmine grinned at him.

'I won't say anything, I promise, but I don't know about the private part. When I asked Gerald if he'd seen you, he told me you were probably canoodling in the kitchen with Nikki. That's a nice word, isn't it—canoodling?'

'Gerald's got a smart mouth,' Nikki said bitterly, but a light brush of David's fingers across her arm stopped her getting really riled.

'I'll see you tomorrow,' he said, then he took her hand and lifted it to his lips, kissed the back of it, then returned it to her. 'Until then,' he added, and he followed his niece out the door.

He did see her the following day, and she him, but it was in work-related capacities. The sunny weekend had brought on flares of disease in two of the unit's SLE patients. One was admitted to the ward with suspected inflammation of the brain as the little boy had suffered a seizure and was disoriented and very weak.

Nikki was on the ward with another patient when the child was admitted so she heard David ordering blood tests and scans. Then the child's mother, Mary Finch, spotted Nikki and came hurrying towards her, perhaps hoping a familiar face might provide comfort.

'I can't believe it happened,' she said to Nikki, taking the blame, as most parents did, for her son's sudden regression.

Nikki patted her shoulder.

'Flares happen, you know that. A child can be symptom-free for months or even years, then something will trigger the disease and it flares up again.'

'It wasn't the sun—I made him stay inside,' Mrs Finch told her, but Nikki knew exposure to the sun was only one possible trigger, although it was the easiest for parents to avoid so it was always in their minds.

'It's more likely to have been an infection of some kind—something going around at school,' Nikki assured her, then she glanced across to where David was speaking to a staff nurse.

'I think they may be taking Ross up to Radiology,' she told Mrs Finch. 'You'll want to go with him.' She gave the anxious mother another reassuring pat. 'Don't worry. Dr Campbell knows what he's doing. Ross is in good hands.'

She watched as David turned and scanned the room, looking for his patient's mother, then he nodded, almost as if he'd expected to find Nikki there as well. He came towards them and his eyes were so grave Nikki felt a wave of anxiety for the little boy, as well as the usual manifestations caused by David's presence.

'We'll start steroid treatment to reduce the inflammation immediately,' he told Mrs Finch. 'He's had the whole battery of tests before so we've got them as a baseline to use in judging the severity of this incident. We'll start with a brain scan and an EEG. I think he'd like you with him.'

He escorted the woman back to where a porter now waited to wheel the bed away, talking quietly all the time, explaining not only what they were about to do, but why.

It was the last Nikki saw of him, except for a fleeting moment when they passed in Outpatients, and he threw her a wry smile and said, 'So much for catching up with you at work. I think I may be here all night, but perhaps tomorrow?'

Tuesday was a little better, work wise, but Ross Finch was still severely ill and Nikki knew David would be considering other drugs to reduce the inflammation because of the risk of permanent brain damage should the inflammation worsen.

By six o'clock Nikki had her paperwork completed, new

exercise programmes worked out for the children who'd regressed, and a tidy desk for once. She was aware she'd lingered in her office in the hope David might eventually be free to leave the hospital and would suggest a drink somewhere, but when he did appear, looking stern and pale, it was apparent socialising was the last thing on his mind.

'Jasmine's disappeared. Meg just rang. Are you free? Would you mind coming to the house? Meg seems to have some crazy idea you might know where she is.'

And from the look in your eyes you just might share that crazy idea, Nikki thought, picking up her jacket from the back of the chair and slinging it around her shoulders.

Disappointment surged through her. How could he even consider she'd be so irresponsible? She followed him out of the room and across to the lifts, where they rode in silence to the car park.

'When was she last seen?' Nikki asked, digging herself out of her shocked daze with practicality.

'This morning. She told Meg she was going on a sight-seeing trip with Harry, then this afternoon Harry phoned to talk to her.'

Nikki shook her head. There was something very wrong with this scenario. Meg's reaction to Harry made him the very last person she'd let her daughter go off with—apart from the carefully supervised visits to the gym.

She glanced at David and decided this wasn't the moment to raise her doubts. She crossed to her car instead, and drove straight to the tall white house in the sedate square, wondering as she found a parking space not too far away how much life, how much trauma, the serene façades must hide.

David had pulled into the house's allotted space so was waiting for her when she reached the steps. They walked up to the door together, the silence between them stiff with tension.

Lucille must have been watching for them, for the door opened and, with a little cry of, 'Oh, David, thank God you're here,' she threw herself into his arms.

He held her close, then kissed her, and, keeping her clamped to his side with one arm, guided her back into the house.

Nikki's dreams crashed around her feet, the image of their destruction so vivid she was surprised they didn't crackle, like broken china, beneath her shoes.

Lucille led them to the study where Meg, tight-faced with fear, was on the phone.

David crossed to the bar and poured two drinks then handed one to Lucille and set one on the desk near his sister. He raised his eyebrows to Nikki, who shook her head. She'd have enough trouble keeping her mind clear without alcohol adding to the tumult.

David must have felt the same, as he poured himself a club soda and took a long draught before turning to Lucille, who'd subsided into one of the leather armchairs and was nursing her glass in both hands.

'Tell me from the beginning,' he said, propping himself against the desk and speaking softly so Meg could continue her conversation. 'Where was she supposed to be going with Harry and how long was this trip supposed to take?'

Lucille sipped her drink.

'She told Meg that Harry had planned a whole sightseeing tour. Madame Tussaud's, a trip on the river, some museums and other places Jazzy was anxious to see.'

Lucille's glance took in both David and Nikki.

'I don't think Meg took much notice,' she said quietly. 'She's uptight and anxious herself and I think she probably listened and agreed without much consideration. I mean, she didn't even ask for Harry's phone number.'

'She knew I'd have it.' Nikki found herself coming to Meg's defence. 'But if they were going out for the day, why would she need his phone number? He wouldn't be there anyway.'

'It wasn't just for the day,' Lucille explained. 'It was for two days.'

Nikki didn't know whether she felt better or worse.

'So, she wasn't expected home until tomorrow evening? She wouldn't know this panic is going on?' she asked.

Lucille looked puzzled.

'No, I don't suppose she would. In fact, if Harry hadn't phoned to speak to her, we still wouldn't know she wasn't with him.'

'So, she's with someone else, and is probably quite safe. For all her missish airs, she's a sensible kid,' Nikki said stoutly, but neither David nor Lucille seemed relieved by her deduction.

'Paul's coming. He's managed to get on a flight to Tokyo that leaves in an hour, then he'll make a connection there and be in London tomorrow some time. I can't work out the difference but he said he wouldn't be long and I've got the flight numbers in case we have to contact him.'

Tears slid down Meg's cheek as she crossed the room to join them, and Nikki sensed they were relief that her ex-husband was on the way.

'Lucille said Jasmine had planned a two-day excursion,' Nikki reminded her. 'It's not as if she just disappeared without telling you she'd be away.'

Meg glared at her, the look so contemptuous Nikki didn't need the 'It's all your fault,' which followed it to tell her what Meg was thinking.

'Perhaps Nikki is right,' David said. 'We're worrying unnecessarily. For all we know, she'll be back at whatever time she said she would tomorrow. Did you phone the police? What did they say?'

'They're sending someone around, but I know they'll agree with you and tell me I'm worrying unnecessarily.

Unnecessarily? When a fourteen-year-old is lost some-where in London—a sick fourteen-year-old at that!'

Nikki could hear the hysteria in Meg's voice and decided practicality was the best approach.

'You thought she was going with Harry. Did he come here to collect her?'

Meg threw her a scornful look.

'Of course not. You've put all this independence non-sense in her head and she insisted she would take the tube. She's been taking it to and from the gym each day so I imagined she was going there first and they'd go on after that.'

It didn't seem right to Nikki. Could Meg have changed from her over-protective self to someone who didn't check on her daughter's destination so suddenly? Was Meg more depressed than David thought? Ill with depression?

Now wasn't the time to follow up on that, and, although her input wasn't appreciated, she had the least emotional involvement so was probably thinking the most clearly.

'She told you she was going with Harry, but has obvi-ously gone off with someone else. Has she talked about other friends she's made? Perhaps people she's met at the gym?'

Meg scowled at her again, but Nikki was already feeling all the guilt Meg was piling on her. If she hadn't introduced the girl to Harry, to the gym, encouraged her independ-ence—

'The only people she ever talks about are those relations of yours, the crippled one and your brother.'

Nikki was aware of David's gaze swinging her way and knew he was expecting her to bite, but she knew Meg's fear for her daughter had made her strike out, and also knew she must do what she could to allay it.

She stood up and crossed to the phone to dial Cecy's

number and got Andrew, home earlier than his loved one for once.

'No, we haven't seen or heard from her, and you know damn well I wouldn't have condoned any irresponsible behaviour,' he told her.

'I don't think it is irresponsible behaviour,' she replied. 'Jasmine told her mother she'd be away two days, even listed the places they would visit. The only lie we're sure of was the name of the person organising this treat. Could you ask Cecy, when she comes in, if Jasmine spoke of anyone to her—a new friend she'd made, someone special perhaps?'

'I'll do that. Keep in touch and let me know if there's anything I can do,' Andrew told her. 'Hang in there, kid,' he added, and Nikki smiled into the phone.

She phoned Harry next. He snatched up the phone as if he'd been sitting waiting for a call.

'No, Nikki, she was friendly with everyone but I didn't notice anyone special. Tell you what, I'll go over there now and get a list of the regulars who are there when Jasmine and I go, then I'll contact all of them for you. How's that?'

'Wonderful, Harry. Thank you. I'm at Jasmine's house so call me here.'

She hung up and passed on Harry's idea. David nodded, Lucille looked approving, but then she stood up and settled herself close to David against the desk which reduced her approval to ashes. Meg stuck to scowling.

'I imagine that's what your police force will do,' she said. 'You're just making extra work.'

'Perhaps,' Nikki said easily, although she wasn't sure how much energy the police would put into looking for a fourteen-year-old who was absent from home intentionally. 'But I think Harry needed something to do. They get along well and he's already involved because she used him as an excuse.'

Again the why of that excuse bothered her, but it was a minor detail, not something she could pursue at the moment.

'Who else has she met? What else has she done? She planned this, you must see that, Meg. She's gone with someone!'

'We've some Australian friends over here with teenage kids. She's visited them a few times with me, but she always said the boys were freaks, and Janey, the daughter, was an egghead, so I can't believe she'd be with them. And if she was going there, Jill, the mother, would have made the arrangements directly with me.'

Which is what I'd have expected you to do with Harry, Nikki thought, but she didn't say it as David had straightened up and was taking over her role as practical support.

'Give me the number, Meg, and I'll phone them. And the phone numbers of anyone else you've visited.'

Meg looked horrified,

'Then everyone will know!'

It had to be panic talking, Nikki thought, as she dismissed the idea that Meg might be more concerned about appearances than the safety of her daughter.

'Better me doing it than the police,' David said. 'Get your address book.'

A loud summons from the doorbell interrupted the proceedings, and Nikki, relieved to escape the tension in the study, hurried out to answer it.

A stout policeman and his trim uniformed woman partner stood on the doorstep. Nikki introduced herself and led them inside, showing them into the study but hanging back, intending to leave the family alone—perhaps rustle up some food to keep up their carbohydrate loading.

'Stay with us, Nikki,' David said—ordered almost. 'You've been involved with Jasmine since the beginning.'

I'd rather stay because you wanted me beside you, Nikki

thought, but she was certain any romance that might have been developing between them had been killed stone-dead by this upheaval.

She moved back into the room but remained as far from the centre of the action as she could, letting David orchestrate the meeting.

When the police departed, she left the family to discuss what they'd do next and found her way to the kitchen. A foray into the cupboards and refrigerator produced bread and ham. They needed food whether they knew it or not, so she'd make sandwiches. It would give her something to do—apart from looking at David and wondering if they might have taken things further. She found a cutting board, but needed a bread knife, so opened the top drawer in an old oak dresser.

It was a junk drawer, the kind where people throw their odds and ends of bills and paper. Not what she was looking for at all, but the top sheet of paper caught her attention— or, rather, the silver bells at the top of the page, perhaps because of talk of Cecy's wedding, made her look twice.

It was a sample wedding invitation, and entwined between the bells were the initials D and L.

She closed her eyes against a blackness that threatened to drag her into oblivion, then reminded herself she'd known all along—that it had been confirmed when she and David had walked into the house this evening and Lucille had found refuge in his arms.

Sandwiches. People need food. Stick to what you can do, she told herself, and think about everything else later. She buttered bread and spread mustard on it, added the pre-cut slices of ham, then slapped the slices together, clumsily cutting them with a bread and butter knife. Nikki boiled water and made a pot of tea and another of coffee. If they went to waste it didn't matter.

She found a large, lacquered tray and set the snack, with

plates, cups and saucers on it, then carried it through to the study, returning to the kitchen for milk and sugar, although everyone was drinking black coffee by the time she returned.

And eating, although she doubted they were noticing what they ate. Unable to stomach food, she settled by the phone, willing it to ring if only to distract her from her pain. Harry was the first caller, phoning to say he'd had no luck, then Cecy rang, sorry she didn't have anything that would help them. Nikki had decided it was time she left when Cecy phoned again, this time to ask if anyone had spoken to Tom.

'I notice she defers to him when they're on the panel together. She might have talked to him about a friend.'

Nikki thanked her then phoned the hospital, bulldozing her way through the objections of the person on night duty who held the privacy laws sacred.

'He's a patient of mine and might have information about a missing girl. Now are you going to give me the phone number or will I phone Martyn Lennard, the hospital manager, and get him to get the information for me?'

A cold voice read out the digits of the phone number, then Nikki heard the click as the phone was disconnected.

Mr Crowley sounded as if the phone had woken him, his voice both bleary and anxious.

'It's Nikki Barclay from the hospital and I'm sorry to bother you at this time of night, but I really need to speak to Tom.'

'He's not here,' the man replied. 'Although he should be back soon. I'll get him to phone you. What was that, love? Oh, Mrs Crowley said they'll be home at eleven. They were doing that tour of the London Dungeon, the last tour is at five-thirty, then going to a show in town, then home.'

London Dungeons! Nikki felt her heart skip a beat, not

with fear of the dreadful tourist attraction but at the pronoun Mr Crowley had used.

'They?' she asked. 'Who's they, Mr Crowley?'

She sensed, rather than saw, David and Meg move closer to her.

'They? Oh, you mean who's with Tom? I thought you knew, thought that's what you were phoning about. The young Australian lady who's a patient at the same hospital.' Nikki raised her thumb to indicate success, her own relief making it difficult to concentrate on what the man was saying. 'Mrs Crowley was going to phone her mother to make sure it was okay she stayed, but Jasmine said her mother was away on a tour and there was only her uncle and herself at home and he was mostly at work anyway. Shall I get her to phone you or is it Tom you want to talk to?'

'Don't bother either of them,' Nikki said. 'There was a misunderstanding about the arrangements but you've sorted it out. Although I'm sure her mother will want to speak to her in the morning.'

Meg grabbed at the phone but Nikki had already depressed the button.

'Jasmine's safe, but she told another lie,' Nikki said to Meg. 'This time to the Crowleys. Apparently they'd have contacted you to confirm the arrangements but she said you were away. She's safe, Meg. There's no need for any more concern. Will it really make any difference if you speak to her tonight or in the morning?'

David had put his arm around his sister, but from the look on his face he wasn't taking Nikki's advocacy of Jasmine any better than Meg was.

'We'll go and get her, right now!' Meg stormed. 'Going off with I don't know who. Telling me lies.'

Nikki laid the piece of paper with the phone number on it on the desk.

'You'll do what you have to do, I suppose,' Nikki said.

'Mrs Crowley said they're expected home at eleven. Tom's a responsible lad, so I'm sure he won't be late. I suggest you let the police know Jasmine's safe, and perhaps phone the friends you rang earlier. I'll contact Harry and my brother.'

David reached for the phone and Nikki walked towards the door, not looking back when he said her name.

'Good morning!'

David's greeting jolted Nikki as she approached the lifts in a stupor made up in equal measure of sleeplessness and unrequited love.

And the smile he gave her caused even more ructions.

'You ran away last night before we could thank you.'

Nikki looked into his eyes, then dropped her head and studied his shiny shoes.

'You didn't have much to thank me for, apart from some long hours of anxiety. Meg was right. If I hadn't interfered in Jasmine's life none of this would have happened.'

'Hey,' he said, using a strong forefinger beneath her chin to force her head up so he could see her face. 'I asked you to interfere in Jasmine's life—and it's been the best thing that's happened to her. Okay, so she did the wrong thing telling lies about her little adventure, and I've no idea why she resorted to such a devious strategy, but nothing will take away the confidence you've given back to her.'

He smiled and she felt her heart breaking all over again, and when he whispered, 'Thank you, Nikki,' and bent to once again brush that so-seductive kiss across her lips, she knew the blood was seeping out.

She backed away from him—knowing she had to ignore that kiss, accept it as nothing more than another gesture of his appreciation.

'What happened after I left? Was she dragged kicking and screaming from Tom's house at eleven, or did Meg content herself with a furious phone call? Not that I could blame her for her anger.'

David's eyebrows twitched into a half-frown, as if the conversation wasn't what he'd expected.

'I persuaded Meg to let the matter rest for the night. After all, why should Jazzy have a disturbed night preparing to face an irate mother? Not that she didn't deserve a few tremors of guilt, but, hell, she's only a kid.'

Nikki felt relieved for Jasmine's sake, and for the Crowleys, who probably didn't want to be fielding late-night phone calls.

'Did Meg speak to her this morning?'

David smiled.

'If you can call a tight-lipped order to return home forthwith speaking to her, then, yes, I guess she did. Jazzy's punishment for the deception will be to miss out on what Tom had planned to show her today.'

'And possibly be grounded for life,' Nikki finished, pressing the button to summon the lift as other early staff crossed the car park towards them.

David stood back to let her and another three women enter first, then moved in, and actually manoeuvred so he was standing beside her.

It doesn't mean anything, she told herself. Politeness, nothing more!

And when it seemed her body needed something to dampen its erratic behaviour, she reminded it of the wedding invitation.

The lift disgorged them into Outpatients, and as they walked towards the suite of offices and treatment rooms that housed the rheumatology unit Nikki realised there was more trouble looming.

Meg had obviously neglected to say, 'Come straight home,' to her daughter, for there, propped outside her door, were a defiant-looking Jasmine and a wary-faced Tom.

'Come home with me, please, Uncle David,' Jasmine begged. 'Please! I can't face Mum on my own. You know how she'll go on.'

Nikki understood how Jasmine felt and could see the indecision on David's grave face.

'You did the wrong thing, Jazzy,' he said gently, 'now you have to take the consequences. I've some very sick children who need my attention this morning. I can't just walk out of here or interfere between you and your mother.'

'Then could Nikki come? Could you spare her for an hour?'

That would go down well with Meg, Nikki thought, but she said nothing, until the one question she'd wanted to ask since the saga began suddenly popped into her head.

'Why did you say you were going with Harry?' she asked Jasmine. 'I mean, why Harry and not Tom—or, if you were telling a lie anyway, why not say Cecy and Andrew?'

Jasmine threw her a scornful look that had so much of her mother in it, Nikki was startled.

'Because I knew Mum would let me go with Harry!' The reply was laden with sarcasm. 'Ever since Mum discovered his uncle's a duke or a lord or something, Harry's become acceptable. If I said I was going with Tom, she'd have said no.'

Nikki shook her head. Apparently, even in egalitarian Australia, social snobbery could still exist.

David looked from Jasmine to Tom, who wasn't by so much as an eyelid blink betraying how he felt about that statement.

'I'm sorry, Tom,' David said, apologising for his sister, then he took out his wallet and withdrew a note, offering it to Tom.

'Would you mind taking Jazzy home in a cab? Her mother will call the police again if she's not there soon.'

Tom waved away the money.

'I was going to take a cab from here anyway,' he said. 'I've got enough money.'

Put the note away, Nikki willed, and she smiled when David slid it straight back into his pocket.

'He'd suffered enough humiliation,' she said as they watched the pair walk towards the front entrance. 'And, although I haven't seen him facing up to an irate parent, I don't think Meg will get rid of Tom too easily. He'll probably provide Jasmine with better protection than either you or I.'

'Either you or I?' David repeated, looking at her with a quizzical gleam in his eyes. 'Do you suppose we could change that to a "you and I", perhaps get together later today—no, we won't take the risk on that not happening after the chaos of the last few days. How about this evening? Dinner somewhere really special. You're the Londoner, you book. I'll call for you at eight.'

He walked back into his office, leaving Nikki gaping after him.

You and I?

Somewhere special?

Call at eight?

I can wear the dress that makes me beautiful, she thought, and smiled mistily at the porter who happened to be passing at that moment.

CHAPTER ELEVEN

NIKKI walked into her office, shut the door, and, clutching her briefcase to her chest, sank back against it.

'Oh, no, not a "love's young dream" re-enactment.'

Once again, the unexpected sound of Crystal's voice elevated Nikki off the ground.

'You're early again!' she muttered accusingly.

Crystal smiled.

'No, actually, you're late. Late for you, anyway. Even Pat's here, although she's gone to the lab to collect test results so she isn't actually here in person right now.'

Nikki heard the words, even understood them, but they were just that—words—and not important ones at that. She could hold on to her dream a little longer.

'If the soupy expression on your face has anything to do with David Campbell, might I mention a woman called Lucille who seemed to be attached, limpet-like, to his arm on Sunday afternoon?'

'Lucille? Damn, I'd forgotten all about her!' Memories of David hugging Lucille the previous evening ran obligingly through her mind.

'I thought you might have,' Crystal said helpfully.

'But he's asked me out to dinner!' Nikki wailed, in truth thinking more of the promise of his kisses than the dinner invitation.

Crystal waved her to her desk.

'You've got a phone, he's probably still in his office. Get it straightened out.'

'Here? Now? I can't do that! It's personal. He's at work. So am I, for that matter.'

'So what are you going to do?' Crystal asked her. 'Spend the day worrying about it, go out to dinner with him then have your hopes dashed when he invites you to the wedding?'

'Wedding! I saw the wedding invitation! I was tired—forgot about it. Then why…?'

'Ask him?' Crystal insisted.

'Just like that? Say, are you going to marry Lucille? I can't do it.'

'Of course you can,' Crystal told her. 'I'll get through to his extension.'

She pressed the required digits then passed the receiver to Nikki who noticed it was shaking against her ear.

'He's not here and I doubt you'll catch him today,' Claire told her when she managed to quaver out his name. 'He went up to the ward, then was due at a hospital meeting at nine-thirty, and he's leaving the place at twelve. Something about collecting his brother-in-law at the airport.'

Claire must have wondered at the silence for she added, 'You could bleep him,' in a helpful voice.

Nikki thanked her and hung up.

'I've missed him,' she told Crystal and was surprised to see her sister-in-law smile.

'That's really good.' Crystal held up her hand to cut off Nikki's protest. 'I know I made you phone, but this works out much better. If you love the man why give in now? It doesn't matter how close he's come to marrying Lucille, he *hasn't* married her. This is your chance, your night. Go out and enjoy it. Relax, have fun, and if he doesn't realise what he'll be missing out on if he doesn't fall in love with you then he's not worth worrying about.'

Nikki chuckled. It was certainly a novel viewpoint, but, damn it all, the man had asked her out—he must have meant something by it.

She lifted the receiver again, this time to phone Andrew,

who not only knew from day to day where the best food was to be had in London, but could also get a table in any restaurant at a moment's notice.

By the time she left work she was a nervous wreck, although Crystal assured her the distracted running of her fingers through her hair all day had given it a lot more body and she should wear it in that casual, unstyled way that evening.

'He'll love it. Want to run his own fingers through it. Believe me!'

Nikki eyed her doubtfully. If she hadn't listened to Crystal this morning she wouldn't be going through this agony. She'd have left him a message to say dinner was off.

By concentrating very hard on the mechanics of driving, she made it safely home.

This is just an ordinary night out, she told herself. With a colleague.

She spread the lavender dress on her bed and ran a bath. Dinner with a colleague, she repeated as she splashed a generous amount of her favourite perfume into the tub.

'An ordinary night out,' she muttered as she tried to get more mascara on her lashes than on her cheeks.

By five to eight she was ready, standing nervously in her living room, and eyeing the bottle of Scotch she kept for visitors. Perhaps just one nip.

The doorbell saved her having alcohol on her breath, and, with her feet trembling in the new black shoes, she crossed the room to answer it—to open the door and see David, resplendent in a dinner suit, looking so handsome she didn't think she'd be able to breathe all evening, let alone talk or eat or drink.

'You are unbelievably beautiful,' he said, holding out his hand and taking one of hers while his gaze skimmed over her, once, and then again. 'I was struck, you know, by the clown's grey eyes,' he added, in a conversational tone that made Nikki think of both heavenly choirs and chocolate. 'Then the person began to intrigue me.'

He took her other hand and looked deep into her eyes.

'Someone who threw herself wholeheartedly into whatever she undertook to do, who brought joy and laughter to her job and all those whose lives she touched. I wondered what it would be like to be married to such a person, which is when I realised I was falling in love with you.'

Nikki wondered if she should say something, but she didn't want him to let go of her hand, nor did she want to stop the heavenly choir.

'I'd thought I was finished with love,' he continued, 'and, after twenty years without practice, had no idea how to begin a courtship, so if I've seemed confused and inept, forgive me, Nikki.'

Me forgive you? You confused and inept?

She shook her head to clear the echoes, and saw him smile.

'I've done it all wrong, haven't I?' he said. 'I should have wined and dined you first then told you how I felt. Come on, we'll start again. I've a car and driver waiting for us. Are you ready? Do you need a coat? Meg always dashes back into the house at least three times before she leaves. Did I tell you Paul has arrived, and, although it happened without your conniving, Miss Organiser, I think they're really talking for the first time in years.'

She could tell from the way he strung his sentences together that he was now even more nervous than she was—if that was possible. But although everything he'd said had made her heart sing, his talk of Meg had reminded her of something she had to clear up.

'What about Lucille?' she asked him.

He looked puzzled.

'Lucille? Oh, you mean where is she while this reunion

is taking place? She and Jazzy have gone out on the town—on a night sightseeing tour. With Desmond, Paul's brother, who flew over as support to him. And Tom as well. Apparently Tom stood his ground, which you need to do with Meg. I do hope Paul's realised that by now.'

He sounded so anxious about his ex-brother-in-law that Nikki wanted to laugh, but the Lucille question remained unresolved and she wasn't going to listen to angel voices singing in her head all night, then find out he was still attached to someone else.

'I didn't mean where is Lucille, but what about you and her? And marriage?'

Now he looked downright shocked.

'I'm not going to marry Lucille!' He frowned at her as if to make sure she knew he was displeased. 'I thought we sorted all that out ages ago.'

Ages ago?

'Does Lucille know that?' Nikki persisted, remembering the invitation.

'Of course she does. In fact, one of the reasons she came over was to see me and let me know she's going to get married. Turns out it's to Desmond, Paul's brother. They knew each other ages ago and apparently have been trying to get Paul and Meg back together then fell in love themselves.'

It took some time to absorb—time David took shameless advantage of by leaning forward and pressing light kisses against her neck.

Which made her breathless all over again.

'Dinner. Car and driver,' she managed to croak as the kisses reached a point beneath her ear that must have been the most erogenous piece of skin in her entire body.

'You're right,' he said, straightening up immediately, although his voice wasn't much better than hers.

'I'll get my things,' she said, and tried to move away

then realised he was still holding both her hands. 'If you'll
let me go for one minute.'

He did, but only while she collected her evening bag and
a warm wrap, then he took possession of them both again,
so they walked out to the car joined like a couple in a
skater's waltz.

The driver leapt out to open the door, and David helped
her in, tucking the filmy layers of the lavender dress around
her legs, murmuring 'beautiful,' under his breath, although
whether he meant the dress or herself, Nikki wasn't sure.

He walked around the car and slipped in beside her.

'Where to?' the driver asked and Nikki told him, then
she sat back, her hand warm in David's, and let the fairy
tale unfold.

Andrew had recommended Scott's, a restaurant Nikki
knew by name but had never visited. The decor was nearly
as overwhelming as David's declarations had been earlier,
and she gasped with pleasure as she took in the tall column
of water and the elegant, curved staircase which seemed to
reflect the water in its glassy finish.

The food was equally impressive, and the company—

She couldn't find the words to describe the company.
Though she knew words to describe the man, his good
looks, his politeness, the little smile that tugged at her heart,
and the feel of his hand when it covered hers. What defied
description was the atmosphere between them—the right-
ness of it all.

Magic came close. She'd make do with that. And in the
meantime there was so much to learn about him, so many
things to discover, like how he set his cutlery down on his
plate so precisely it didn't make a clatter, or the way his
eyes could smile at her over the rim of a glass as he took
a sip.

'I think they might be wanting to close up,' he said,
much later, when they'd lingered for hours over coffee and

chocolates, sharing ideas and opinions, arguing placidly over food tastes, agreeing about the United Nations, touching on so many subjects as they began to learn about each other.

The driver was summoned from wherever drivers went while diners dined, and once again David tucked her into the car as if she were a delicate piece of Dresden china. When he took his seat beside her, he regained possession of her hand and held it tightly as if he would never let it go.

She knew instinctively he'd make no other move, knew he wasn't a man to steal a kiss and possibly embarrass both her and the driver, although she was reasonably certain these drivers had seen more than stolen kisses.

Should she ask him in? Suggest coffee when they'd already had too much caffeine?

She let her fingers curl around his and returned the pressure of his hand, then caught herself swallowing a yawn.

'It's okay,' David told her. 'I've been stifling them myself. I don't know if it's relief that I've finally spoken to you about how I feel, or the accumulation of the sleepless and emotional nights I've had lately, but I'm exhausted. Would you be offended if I drop you home and not come in? I promise we'll have lunch together tomorrow and plan stage two.'

'Stage two?' Nikki echoed.

Now he did lean towards her and steal a kiss.

'The seduction scene,' he whispered, and her heart thumped so loudly she wondered if the driver might hear it.

'It's probably a good idea,' she said, then realised she'd answered the wrong sentence.

'I know,' he murmured, his breath tickling in her ear and sending shivers across her skin.

'I meant going straight home,' she said severely. 'It's

after two and my boss will expect to see me working tomorrow, not dozing on a therapy table.'

'As long as he sees you for lunch, he won't care what you do,' David assured her as the car pulled into her drive.

He told the driver to wait and alighted himself to open her door, then escort her into her flat. Where he wrapped his arms around her and fitted her body tidily into his.

'I love you, Nicole Barclay,' he declared, then he sealed the words with a kiss.

A long kiss that sent shock waves of pleasure reverberating through Nikki's body, promising so much delight it was only with great difficulty she let him disentangle himself and move away from her.

'I'll try to see you in the morning some time,' he promised, dropping little kisses on the top of her tousled hair. 'But otherwise one in the café?'

She nodded, rendered speechless by the power of that kiss, and watched him walk out the door, closing it noiselessly behind him.

Although she'd been certain the excitement quivering in her body would keep her awake all night, the opposite happened and she fell into a deep, restful sleep, and slept through the alarm she rarely needed, waking only when the insistent ringing of the phone broke through into a dream of David and seduction, and, in the peculiar way of dreams, Cheshire cheese.

'Why aren't you at work?' Crystal demanded. 'David was in earlier, looking for you, then, fortunately, he was called up to the ward. Young Ross Finch is very ill. Are you sick?'

Nikki pulled herself together, did a quick inner survey of herself and said, 'No, I'm fine. Really good. I just slept in.'

'I won't ask why,' Crystal told her. 'Not after seeing the smug smirk on our temporary boss's face. Have fun?'

'We went to dinner and that's all,' Nikki protested, then realised she should be getting ready for work, not arguing on the phone. 'If he comes again, stall him. I won't be long.'

She hung up on Crystal's next question, then hurriedly washed and dressed.

'He hasn't been back and I took your early appointment,' Crystal told her when she finally arrived in the office. 'I wanted to see that patient about new splints anyway. You can have my space next week.' She then cocked an eyebrow at the plastic-draped suit Nikki had slung over her shoulder. 'You collecting his dry-cleaning already?'

It took Nikki a minute to catch on. She swung the suit off her shoulder and hung it on the hook behind the door.

'This? No, it's Gerald's. For my therapy session this afternoon.'

Crystal nodded understandingly then dashed off to her next appointment, leaving Nikki to check her programme for the day and make sure she was free for lunch.

Not that David was! He phoned at twelve to say he was waiting for another specialist he'd called in to see Ross and, as he didn't think he'd get back downstairs for the rest of the day, he'd phone her later to make arrangements for the evening.

Then, in an act of bravery unparalleled in her experience, he murmured 'I love you' into the phone, in spite of knowing that no hospital conversation was ever sacred and that ten extensions could have heard the declaration.

Not quite as brave, Nikki contented herself with a feeble, 'Me too,' which wasn't, she realised later, even grammatically correct.

She had lunch with Crystal, and recounted the previous

evening in minute detail, smiling as she relived the magic of just being with the man she loved.

'Okay, I've heard enough,' Crystal said at last. 'You'd better get ready for your therapy session and I'm going out to buy an umbrella.'

'An umbrella? Have you lost yours?' Nikki asked, and Crystal grinned at her.

'No, it's an engagement present for David. I want to have it ready when the big announcement is made.'

She whisked away, leaving Nikki staring bemusedly after her, wondering where an umbrella fitted into the conversation. Or into the category of engagement presents!

Still puzzling, she changed into Gerald's suit, knotted the bright tie she'd chosen from his meagre wardrobe around her neck, then wet her hair and slicked it back so she looked like a reasonably handsome chap.

The therapy session went well, the little ones trying extra hard to follow 'Simon's' orders, laughing with delight when she fooled them. It was hard work for her as she danced around the room, every movement she asked them to mimic designed to move the joints through their full range of motion.

'Okay, some quiet time. Simon says lie on your mats and have a rest.' There was only one programme that needed modification, and she picked out that parent.

'Mrs Blythe, I'd like to make a few alterations to Jamie's home programme. Do you mind waiting a few minutes? It won't take me long.'

She said goodbye to the other parents, then, intent on getting back to her office, she backed out the door, calling 'Simon says wave goodbye,' to her little charges.

And stepped slap-bang into a solid, bulky body.

'What the hell?' a chocolaty voice murmured in the vicinity of her ear, while two firm hands gripped her waist.

'We were playing Simon says,' she said feebly, turning in time to see the double take as David recognised her.

'I might have known,' he said, grinning at her in such a funny way she could feel her bones melting. Then the grin faded and his eyes grew intent, and she held her breath as his head tilted towards her and his lips brushed against hers with that tantalising touch she knew she'd never again be able to resist.

Nikki gave in to her feelings and flung her arms around his neck, responding to the kiss with all the passion she'd been hiding because she'd feared this was another case of love that would cause her grief.

'I doubt this public display of affection, touching though it is, is doing David's reputation much good.'

Crystal's dry remark brought Nikki to her senses, and she sprang away from David then had to clutch at the door jamb to steady herself.

'I was coming to tell you I'd finished earlier than I expected, and to suggest we grab a bite to eat on the way home,' David said, obviously less affected by the kiss than she had been. 'Perhaps we could pick up a take-away and eat at your place.'

Nikki looked into his eyes and saw both love and excitement.

'Coward!' she teased, and he shook his head.

'No such thing. I think you look fantastic in a suit. I'm more concerned about keeping my hands off you and the British rules of decency, given that you're such a reserved and reticent lot!'

CHAPTER TWELVE

'I CAN'T go home without you!' David complained when the cricket Tests had finished and Mark had returned from Hollywood.

'You'll have to,' Nikki told him, although her heart ached at the thought of losing him—if only temporarily. 'There's no way I can leave until Mark's chosen a replacement for me and he or she know the kids and is comfortable with the work.'

They were sitting on their favourite bench in the park, although the sky was grey and the wind chilly—the warm days of summer a memory as autumn blew towards them. Nikki broke the crust off her sandwich and crumbled it into smaller pieces for the ducks.

'It's not as if we'll be apart for long. I'm coming out in a month for Meg's wedding, then you'll be back here right after Christmas for...'

'Say it, Nikki,' he said, in the deep voice that still sent shivers down her spine. 'Say "our wedding".'

She forgot the ducks and turned to face him, studying his dear, familiar face as the wonder of what had happened between them once again threatened to overwhelm her.

'I find it so hard to believe,' she muttered. 'I keep thinking I'll wake up and discover it's all a dream.'

'Like this is an illusion?' David asked, leaning towards her and planting a very real kiss on her lips.

Something nudging at her leg brought her back to the real world and she looked down to see a duck, angry at her sudden neglect, demanding more food.

'That's real enough,' she admitted, as he trailed his fingers along the line of her chin. 'And if you don't stop tormenting me I'll forget my obligation to Mark, and the children, and stow away in your suitcase.'

'Now, there's an interesting scenario,' he teased, then he stood up and drew her to her feet, walking back to the hospital with her and coming in to the unit although he was no longer working there.

Nikki understood. He was due to depart in less than twenty-four hours, and it seemed as if every minute they spent apart was wasted.

'Get out of here and let her do some work,' Mark greeted him as they dawdled their way through Outpatients. 'In fact, come up to the ward with me. The young Finch boy is back in again. There must be something wrong with the protocol we're using.'

Nikki watched as the man she loved switched personae— from the lover to the doctor in the blink of an eye.

'I'll see you later,' she said, and, although he nodded, and even smiled at her, she knew she'd already lost him, the faint crease between his eyebrows a sure sign he was listing what he remembered of the treatment and seeking alternatives in the recesses of his mind.

But that night his thoughts were all for her, and when they parted the next morning—she going reluctantly to work while he headed for the airport and his home on the other side of the world—it was with the memory of their love-making warm and secure in both their hearts.

'There was snow in the night.'

Nikki snuggled deeper into the warmth of her bed.

'I don't want a weather forecast, Mum. I want a long-acting anaesthetic so I can wake up in Australia in about a week, married to David and ready to get on with real life.'

'Weddings are part of real life,' her mother protested.

'I've put a cup of tea on your bedside table; don't knock it over when you sit up.'

The ordinariness of it all brought Nikki's head out from beneath the bedclothes.

'Is that all you can say to your only daughter on her wedding morning? Don't knock over the cup of tea?'

Her mother smiled placidly.

'What do you want me to say? That David's a lucky man to be getting a wonderful woman for his wife? That he's also a fine and honourable man who will share equal responsibility with you for making your marriage work? Perhaps a little homily about happiness needing as much tending and nurturing as my roses?'

She came towards the bed and bent to wrap her arms around Nikki's shoulders.

'You know all that, and more. You've always been willing to work hard to achieve your goals. Marriage is no different to any other job so go into it with the same joy and optimism you took to the clinic. Use your special talents, your energy and enthusiasm, to keep the love you share fresh and beautiful, and your life together challenging and interesting.'

Nikki gazed at her mother in awe.

'Is that how you see me?' she asked.

Her mother nodded, then smiled and added huskily, 'You mightn't have played cricket for England, but we're far prouder of you than we could ever say.'

Nikki sniffed back a few silly tears and grinned.

'Having the reserve and reticence I missed out on!' she teased. Then she caught sight of the wedding dress, hung in its pristine whiteness on the door of the wardrobe, and the enormity, not of marriage, but of the day ahead struck her and she was tempted to retire beneath the bedclothes again. 'Oh, Mum, why did I decide to do this full-scale wedding business? Why not a register office? Why didn't we elope? David wouldn't have minded.'

Mrs Barclay chuckled.

'As I remember, it was something to do with that enthusiasm of yours. And possibly the pleas of a couple of little girls—three if you count Jazzy, though she certainly wouldn't want to be classed as a child.'

'Susan and Emma!' Nikki sighed. 'How could I resist when they begged to be flower-girls and have worked like little Trojans on their exercises for the past few months so I wouldn't renege?'

She settled back against the pillows and drank the lukewarm tea. She looked at the dress again and shook her head. Then she remembered Susan and Emma's delight when she'd agreed to have them in the wedding party—their excitement when they'd come for fittings and gazed in awe at their therapist transformed by bridal finery.

And thought of David, and wondered what he'd think of her in the long, simply styled dress of soft white velvet. Thought of David...

The snow had been swept from the path leading into the cathedral, but it had settled on the trees, and shrubs, and old stone building, transforming the area into a picture-book scene. Nikki stood for a moment, enjoying the sheer beauty of it all, then her father reminded her to lift her dress so it didn't get wet and she took a deep breath and walked resolutely towards the front of the building.

Her supporters had arrived earlier and were waiting in the porch, two excited flower-girls, both clad in long, dark blue velvet frocks and holding small baskets of rose petals in their hands. Jasmine, in paler blue, was giving last-minute instructions to the little ones. Leaning awkwardly down, she adjusted the coronet of roses on Susan's head, then checked on Emma's. She looked up as Nikki approached.

'Wow!' she said simply, and gave a beaming smile of approval and a quick thumbs-up sign.

Meg, there to keep an eye on the young ones, smiled tearfully at Nikki, then reached up to touch one of the same tiny white rosebuds she wore twisted into her hair in place of a hat or veil.

'You look beautiful,' she murmured. 'I'm so happy for you both.'

Nikki heard the words but her sense of unreality was so great she barely comprehended this first admission that Meg might actually approve of her brother's choice of bride.

Then the music began, familiar from a rehearsal during which she'd joked about the folly of all this pageantry! She felt the slight pressure of her father's hand on hers. Susan and Emma, coached by Meg, fell into line behind her, then Jazzy, her sticks bound in white ribbon and trimmed with the same white rosebuds they all wore in their hair.

'We're on,' her father whispered, the huskiness of his voice revealing his emotion.

'Okay, let's do it,' she said to him and stepped out, remembering to go slowly—to step then pause—seeing the back of David's head as he stood with Paul at the front of the church, as far away as the wicket at Lords must seem for a batsman walking out to the centre for the first time.

He didn't turn until she was one pace from him, then he looked at her and smiled.

'Dressing up again, Nikki?' he murmured, as her father shuffled her into position.

She looked at the man she was about to marry, read the love and steadfastness in the beautiful blue of his eyes, and suddenly the meaning of the day became abundantly clear.

'No,' she said softly, aware the minister was waiting to begin but needing to answer the man she loved. 'This time it's for real!'

Harlequin Romance®

Delightful
Affectionate
Romantic
Emotional

Tender

Original

Daring
Riveting
Enchanting
Adventurous
Moving

Harlequin Romance®—
capturing the world you dream of...

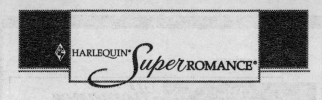

...there's more to the story!

Superromance.
A *big* satisfying read about unforgettable
characters. Each month we offer *six* very different
stories that range from family drama to adventure
and mystery, from highly emotional stories to
romantic comedies—and much more! Stories
about people you'll believe in and care about.
Stories too compelling to put down....

Our authors are among today's *best* romance
writers. You'll find familiar names and talented
newcomers. Many of them are award winners—
and you'll see why!

**If you want the biggest and best
in romance fiction, you'll get it
from Superromance!**

Emotional, Exciting, Unexpected...

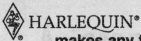

HARLEQUIN®
makes any time special—online...

eHARLEQUIN.com

your romantic
books

♥ Shop online! Visit Shop eHarlequin and discover a wide selection of new releases and classic favorites at great discounted prices.

♥ Read our daily and weekly Internet exclusive serials, and participate in our interactive novel in the reading room.

♥ Ever dreamed of being a writer? Enter your chapter for a chance to become a featured author in our Writing Round Robin novel.

your romantic
life

♥ Check out our feature articles on dating, flirting and other important romance topics and get your daily love dose with tips on how to keep the romance alive every day.

• • • • • •

• • • • • •

your
community

♥ Have a Heart-to-Heart with other members about the latest books and meet your favorite authors.

♥ Discuss your romantic dilemma in the Tales from the Heart message board.

your romantic
escapes

♥ Learn what the stars have in store for you with our daily Passionscopes and weekly Erotiscopes.

♥ Get the latest scoop on your favorite royals in Royal Romance.

Medical Romance™

LOVE IS JUST
A HEARTBEAT AWAY!

New in North America, **MEDICAL ROMANCE**
brings you four passionate stories every month...
each set in the action and excitement of big-city
hospitals and small-town medical practices.
Devoted doctors, sophisticated surgeons,
compassionate nurses—you'll meet this
group of dedicated medical professionals
in this thrilling series. Their fast-paced
world and intense emotions are
guaranteed to provide you
with hours and hours of
reading pleasure.

To find out
more about
this exciting new
series, contact our toll
free customer service
number: 1-800-873-8635 and
reference #4542 when calling.
You won't find it in bookstores!

HARLEQUIN®
Makes any time special ®